JOURNEYMAN

JOURNEYMAN

MARC BOJANOWSKI

GRANTA

Granta Publications, 12 Addison Avenue, London W11 4QR

First published in Great Britain by Granta Books 2015

A CIP catalogue record for this book is available from the British Library.

1 3 5 7 9 10 8 6 4 2

ISBN 978 1 78378 251 2
eISBN 978 1 78378 252 9

Typeset by Avon DataSet Ltd, Bidford on Avon, B50 4JH
Printed and bound by CPI Group (UK) Ltd, Croydon, CR0 4YY

MIX
Paper from
responsible sources
FSC
www.fsc.org
FSC® C020471

for my parents,
with love and gratitude

1

The man stands on the roof of the mansion enveloped by an amorphous cloud of atomized paint. He waves a spray gun back and forth over the stucco chimney stack, and with each pass of the gun new flecks materialize where others have disappeared, leaving him surrounded by an aura of dazzling light.

Down in the courtyard, William Nolan Jackson watches the iridescent cloud expand and contract beneath the high noon sun. He watches the forms it takes around the painter's movements, and he studies the colors flashing at its periphery, flashing as if some meaning exists there, playfully hidden, or hiding. There's a pulse to the paint cloud, an itinerant ease to its transitions that Nolan admires. It is, for him, a thing of beauty.

—Don't see that every day, now, do you? a voice says.

Nolan turns to find the job site's foreman standing beside him.

—No, sir, he agrees. You don't.

The foreman crosses his arms against his chest, lifts his chin, and tilts his head to the side. He squints to see the cloud better. Then, deadpan, he says to Nolan:

—You want a lawn chair or something? Maybe an iced tea and a bucket so you can put your boots up?

Before Nolan can respond, the painter's compressor switches on, loud and jarring, and the foreman steps forward and raises his hands to his face so that the ends of his fingers press together at the bridge of his nose and his thumbs tripod along his jaw.

—Hey, he yells at the house painter. I'm going to the deli for a sandwich. You want anything?

When the painter turns, the cloud turns with him. It moves slowly, with a systemic elegance. The painter rests the spray gun in the crook of his elbow, his eyes hidden behind a pair of dark sunglasses freckled with old paint. He reaches into the front pocket of his splattered coveralls and removes a crushed pack of brand-name cigarettes.

Behind him, Nolan notices, the sky is vast and white and blue. Wispy strands of cirrus extend into reflections cast in the window banks of a high-rise casino-hotel down on the Las Vegas Strip, and from the rooftop of another sky-rise the long arm of a yellow crane sweeps evenly over the desert cityscape. Nolan watches the painter place a bent cigarette at the corner of a wry smile and raise a disposable plastic lighter to his face. To the foreman, the man says:

—Yeah. Get me a chocolate milk and a nudie mag.

The last of his words are lost to flames.

When he strikes the lighter, the paint cloud explodes, rattling the courtyard windows in their casings. Caught on fire, the man stands in place flailing and screaming, lifting one foot and then the other while swiping at his face and his head like a harried marionette in pantomime. Nolan steps forward, amazed. The color of the flames dull in the brightness of the day. Before Nolan can say or do anything, the painter's knees buckle, his body collapses to the tiles, and he falls from the second-story roof, flames whipping about his body.

Nolan is at the man's side, swatting out the fire with his work shirt, when the foreman, breathing heavily, shoves him away. The foreman drops to his knees beside the man. Nolan's ears ring and he can feel the desert sun warm on his bare shoulders. He sees a mason hurrying over with a five-gallon bucket of water. A tile setter hustles beyond the compressor noise, already pressing a cell phone to one ear and his free hand to the other. Seeing the compressor's yellow extension cord, Nolan reaches down and yanks it from an outdoor wall plug. Suddenly, the job site is quiet. The mason runs up and lifts the bucket but the foreman raises his hand and stops him from dumping the water on the painter.

—No, he says. The lye.

The mason pours the bucket out on the concrete walkway and runs to a nearby spigot.

Nolan steps toward the painter, who lies flat on his stomach, his arms straight at either side, his blistered palms upturned. The burns on his neck range from purple to red to black. Pressed to the dirt, his cheek glistens, and colorful bits of discarded wire-stripping stick to the pocks in his face. Tiny flames linger along the loops of his sneaker laces.

Nolan knows the man isn't dead, but he doesn't know the extent to which he's injured or what to do in the span of time before someone who will know arrives. He feels helpless, the feeling he despises most.

The foreman, careful not to place his hands on the man's singed coveralls, leans over the painter.

—Set still, buddy, Nolan hears him say. Help's coming.

When the foreman speaks, a silver filling glints at the back of his mouth, and because of it Nolan notices the sunlight spilling over the painter's body. He steps back and unfurls his work shirt and holds it up best he can as a shade.

—Come on, man, the foreman whispers to the painter as the mason returns with the bucket of water and a handful of rags. Hang in there.

Noon the next day Nolan arrives at University Medical Center to find the foreman and an electrician from the site smoking cigarettes in the shade of a cloth awning. The men stand on either side of a cylindrical concrete ashtray, down a gently sloped ramp from a pair of sliding glass doors that open to the hospital lobby. A camera, the size of a small black bird, sits above the center of the door. The foreman and the electrician raise and lower their hands to their faces and exhale smoke into a hot, dry afternoon breeze that occasionally threatens the electrician's comb-over. When Nolan reaches the brushed concrete ramp, the foreman says:

—Well, well, well, if it ain't the Lonely Ranger.

—How's he holding up? Nolan asks.

—Fucker survives Afghanistan to come home and fall off a roof.

The electrician lowers his face and bites his lower lip and reaches up to smooth down his thinning hair. None of the men looks at each other.

—Nah, the foreman continues, he'll be all right. Doc says his back's busted from the fall, but he'll walk again with some rehab.

—What about the burns?

—The ones on his neck and hands are pretty bad—

—Tell him about his forehead, the electrician interrupts.

The foreman coughs up a floppy lozenge of green phlegm

and spits it at the base of a nearby oleander shrub in bloom. Pink blossoms.

—You tell him.

—They grafted some skin up off his ass and glued it to his forehead, the electrician says, tapping his forehead with his middle finger, his cigarette protruding from his curled hand, a stupid grin on his pasty, unlikable face.

—Old butthead, we're calling him.

—You're calling him, the foreman says, taking a puff on his cigarette.

Nolan stares into the electrician's eyes until the man's eyes waver and he looks away.

—What room's he in? Nolan asks the foreman.

—421. His wife's up there, sitting with him. Go on up and introduce yourself.

The foreman lifts his fist to show Nolan the end of his cigarette.

—We'll be up in a bit.

The house painter lies swaddled in gauze and face down in a bed designed for the injuries he's sustained. His wife, a petite woman in her late twenties, sits in an armchair beside the bed. She points a remote control in the direction of a muted television, mounted high on the wall opposite. They have the room to themselves, and a colorful bouquet of flowers and a GET WELL SOON card adorn the particle-board dresser in the far corner of the room. A Mylar balloon presses against the ceiling. The tiny bell at the end of its ribbon lies nestled at the center of a stack of hospital pillows and folded blankets. The room smells of ammonia and synthetic citrus, and the regular beeps from the monitors are subtly oppressive.

Nolan stands at the doorway, hat in hand, waiting to be acknowledged, but the woman is concentrating on the buttons on the remote. He doesn't know the house painter outside of work, and even at work, not that well. He remembers one day when, at a burrito lunch the foreman bought for all the workers on site out of his own pocket, the painter shared two stories about his service overseas. The first concerned a raid on a hillside village of mud huts. A child cowered in a corner. The entire thing witnessed through the disorientating green of night-vision goggles. The second story briefly chronicled a spring snowmelt. The bleating of goats, stranded by a flooded river, reached the painter at the makeshift mountain outpost he and his fellow soldiers had constructed. They stayed at the outpost until summer, he said. They drank goat's milk, still warm, and scoped the valley to no avail for a hidden patch of marijuana, the sweet scent of which was brought by the wind each evening to the young men, far from home.

But Nolan can't recall the man having ever mentioned a wife.

A streak of light across the room's only window brings Nolan back. In the distance, smoggy Mojave.

The painter's wife scoots to the edge of the armchair, and holding the remote with both hands she shoves it adamantly in the direction of the television. Nolan takes a quiet step back from the doorway. The day the painter shared his two stories, a teenage apprentice plumber asked him if he'd ever killed anyone in combat. The gathered tradesmen, sitting on buckets or against the mansion in the shade, looked at their food or their feet. The apprentice, though, looked the painter in the eye. Nolan watched the painter tilt a glance to those around him and say, almost laughing:

—You see how easy that shit just fell off his tongue?

One or two of the men nodded, and the foreman said:

—I blame video games. That, and pornography.

—What's pornography got to do with it? the electrician with the comb-over asked.

—I don't know, the foreman answered. I just thought it sounded good.

—Did you? the apprentice asked the painter.

—You don't understand this yet, Nolan said then, his voice almost cracking he spoke so seldom, but you're being rude.

—He's the one telling war stories. The apprentice pointed at the painter.

—Those aren't war stories, son, the foreman interjected. We're just talking about places we've been.

—Even if I had, the painter said finally, I wouldn't tell a shit-mover like you.

—No reason to be insulting about it, the apprentice said.

—Sure there is.

In the hospital room, the painter's wife shoves the remote at the television one last time before slumping back in the chair and letting her hands fall in her lap. Nolan steps back into the shadows of the hallway as the woman's hair falls across her face and her features scrunch and her shoulders begin to shudder. He looks down at his hands, holding his hat, and he turns and leaves.

Later that day, at a gas station quick mart, Nolan sets two 22-oz aluminum cans of domestic beer and five microwaved chicken tamales wrapped in plastic wrap on the counter.

—And a half pint of that top-shelf brown, he says to the clerk.

The clerk waves the bottle of whiskey in front of the scanner several times before the coded strip registers with a beep. Above her left shoulder, a small colored monitor displays Nolan, captured from three different camera angles. Nolan and each of the empty, stocked aisles.

Outside, Nolan sits in the driver's seat of his truck, parked in one of the quick mart's parking slots, facing the last of the setting sun, with his white Western hat canted against the diminishing star. Parked in the next slot, a dusty, late-model sedan filled with an assortment of belongings all packed in brown grocery sacks. A dream catcher with red and yellow bird feathers dangles from the rearview mirror, held together by duct tape and wire. Nolan watches the reflection of the desert behind him, blue dark, in one of the sedan's side mirrors. Ahead, the final arc of the sun.

Over the next hour, vehicles come and go from the parking stalls around him, but he sits in his '76 Ranger with the windows down, sipping the whiskey and enjoying the cross-breeze when it comes.

When he was a boy, he and his older brother Chance wandered the oak woodlands of the Sierra Nevada foothills hunting rabbit with pellet guns their father had bought for them at Christmas. One morning early, they came upon a shack in the woods. A one-room structure with horizontal siding and a wood-shingle roof. Most of one entire wall was taken up by a French window curtained shut with thick red quilts, sun faded. A rundown windowless van parked in front of the shack. Gray sky reflected in large puddles of brown rainwater.

Chance was ten and Nolan was seven, and as soon as they happened upon the clearing where the shack stood, the older boy dropped to a crouch behind a decaying log and began pumping his rifle. Nolan watched Chance aim at a green bottle of beer that stood by a leg of a chair on the front porch. Knowing, in the time it took Chance to aim, that he would be expected to shoot next. A sweet, foreign-smelling smoke rose from the stone chimney at the back of the shack. Winter, and the boys' jeans soaking wet from walking in the tall grasses after a night of rain.

Chance missed, and Nolan shot next and he toppled the bottle. They went on like this, choosing targets, old yellow-and-black license plates, torn seat backs, seashell wind chimes, all the while Chance working them closer and closer to the curtained window until it was Nolan's turn. The better shot, he missed the window on purpose, but before Chance could shoot, the door to the cabin burst open and three men, set on fire, rushed out to the yard, fell to their knees, and began shoveling fistfuls of mud down their throats to extinguish the flames in their lungs. The last thing Nolan saw before he and Chance ran was the inside of the shack on fire, the flames rising from knocked-over equipment.

They ran all the way home, and when they told their father what had happened their mother called in the fire. Later that evening, house windows dark and reflective, the phone rang in the kitchen and half an hour later their father was driving the boys to the sheriff's department in Placerville. After parking across the street from the office, their father rested his hands on his thighs and said:

—You boys did nothing wrong, so don't act like it.

Nolan watched the keys sway on their ring, the one key still inserted in the truck's ignition. Leaning against the passenger door, Chance tried to stifle his cries, his eyes red and swollen.

—Chance, their father said.

—What?

—What'd I just say?

—We didn't do anything wrong.

—Then why are you crying?

—I don't know.

Nolan looked up at his father as the headlights of an oncoming vehicle shone across his face.

—Then we'll just sit here until you're ready.

First drops of rain on the windshield and the feel of their father's wool flannel on the back of his neck as the man reached over Nolan to rest his hand on Chance's shoulder. Three of them sitting in a row on the plastic bench seat. The cancer already in him.

South of the gas station quick mart, just beyond the entrance ramp to the interstate, a faded billboard advertises an eighteen-hole golf course lined with luxury estates. A small figure waterskis across the glassy turquoise lake at the center of the illustration of the housing tract, the skier leaving in its wake the words *Desert Oasis* inscribed in elegant script. Nolan traces the letters of the words superimposed on that imaginary world. He traces them right to left so they lose meaning and then left to right so they gather it up again. For, impossible as the tranquil lake and the stately homes and the lush green fairway grass may seem in the desert, he knows that what the billboard promises, to some extent, is possible. He's labored on its behalf in this state and others. He's profited from helping to will it into the world.

The upper corner of the billboard is torn to reveal a patch of blinding white space, a torn corner where some individual has reached and wildly inscribed, in black permanent marker, the name:

Nolan checks his mirrors, raises the bottle in a silent toast to the inscription and advertisement both, and then takes a sip of the whiskey.

He stays in this place until daylight fades completely. Observer and participant.

On the night of the burning men, an hour or so after they'd gone to sleep, their father opened the door to the room Nolan shared with Chance and stood in the doorway. Nolan was still awake. His father's form cast in silhouette by the hallway light overhead.

—Dad? Nolan finally said.

—What's up, bud?

—Why were they eating mud?

—What do you mean?

—When they came out of the house, they ate the dirt in the driveway.

His father sighed.

—Do you know, Dad?

—The fire was in their lungs.

—Oh.

—And they thought it would put it out.

—But it didn't?

—No.

—What were they doing in there?

—They were cooking drugs.

—Why?

—Because they chose to.

On the streets and avenues below where Nolan's parked, headlamps course along the undersides of the insulated power lines. Lamp standards flicker on, leaning out over the concrete sidewalks like drooping heliotropes, and living-room windows turn television blue. A dozen beams of white light roam the sky in programmed arcs, centered around a single column of light that emanates from the apex of a substantial black pyramid.

—We didn't shoot the window, Dad.

—I know.

—I swear we didn't.

—I believe you.

—But a pellet could have gone through one of the walls?

—We don't know that for certain.

—But it could have?

—Go to sleep, bud. It's not your fault.

In the time Nolan has been sitting at the station, a vast illuminated grid has surfaced below, the combined light enough to obscure entire galaxies from the night sky.

Down on the Strip, the balmy night air smells of chlorinated water and car exhaust. He parks his truck on the top floor of a massive concrete parking structure and walks down a stairwell that stinks of urine to street level. When he emerges from the stairwell, the artificial light is intense and briefly overwhelming. Immediately caught in the stream of tourists, he happens upon a stumblebum of inebriated bridesmaids. The women tote tall, skinny plastic containers filled with slushy margarita mix.

—Oh, my god, one woman says.

—I know, right? says another.

The women stop ahead of him and assemble to take a group picture. Drunk himself, Nolan weaves purposefully through the crowd into the background of their photograph, touching the brim of his hat as he does and wondering once he's passed if he was captured there with them, to be noticed sometime in their future, that coy cowboy in the brightly lit thoroughfare.

—Sodom and Gomorrah, a street preacher intones, startling Nolan. Cities of the plain.

A few steps on, he overhears one man say to another:

—Way you were squirming in your seat, I figured you either for the flush or a nasty case of worms.

—Should've paid to see which.

—Maybe next time.

He enters the casino where Linda works by a side-entrance corridor lined with tiny storefronts that vend luxury goods from six of the seven continents. The faux-cobblestone flooring is waxed to a high sheen and the ceiling bears a mural of pink and white clouds, shapes too similar to be mere apophenia.

A commotion of slot-machine sounds comes from the far end of the corridor, and cheering erupts from a crowded craps table. Nolan walks carefully from the corridor onto the casino floor, doing his best impression of sober.

—Five point, the stick man monotones at the craps table. Two and three makes five and point.

When Nolan finds her, she's crossing the floor holding a tray laden with glasses and beer bottles. He sits at an empty slot machine and feeds it the occasional quarter while watching her distribute drinks to the gamblers. He likes how she accepts their tips with two taps of the chips on the plastic edge of her cork-lined tray. The pleated black mini-skirt she wears complements her long, toned legs. Her long hair is tied up neatly in a ponytail.

Nolan smiles at her when she notices him, and she winks

back, mindful of the cameras. When her tray is full of empties, she walks over to where he sits. The blinking lights of the slot machine color the white of his Western hat. They glow on the toes of his freshly oiled chukkas.

—I was hoping I might see you tonight, she says.

—You got plans later?

Writing nonsense on her pad, she says:

—I do now.

They meet in a sports bar in a treeless strip mall several blocks from the condominium Linda owns outright, bought with money she inherited when she turned twenty-one, her parents having died of pancreatic and breast cancer within three months of each other when she was ten. A little girl left to be raised by a loving grandmother. Nolan sits watching a car race on the television mounted above the bar. Tinted camera dome above the TV screen. The cars race on a banked asphalt speedway until they're slowed by a minor wreck. The driver of the wrecked car pulls himself through the window of the spun-out car and strides down the bank as the other racers swerve to miss him. He wears a helmet with a visor and a fireproof suit and he walks directly toward the car of the driver who put him there and shakes his gloved fist at him as the fire crew arrives, yellow-orange lights swiveling.

—Idiot, the bartender says, and Nolan nods.

Out the front window of the bar, stark white parking lines glow against the recently sealed asphalt. The lines like a bright white framework that hovers and tilts on an unseen axis in that black void. Nolan watches Linda cross the parking lot on her approach. Long, slow strides over asphalt still warm from the day. She wears her hair down and she's changed into a pair of fitted blue jeans and a soft-pink cashmere sweater. Stylish and practical shoes. When she enters the bar, Nolan stands and offers her his stool while steadying himself against the bar.

—You look nice, he says.

She hangs her leather wallet on a hook beneath the bar.

—Wait until you see what I've got on underneath.

Later, she lies naked with her head on his shoulder and his leg cradled between her thighs. The louvered blinds of her bedroom window are partially turned against the light of the community swimming pool two stories below, and shadows and light ripple across the skip-troweled ceiling, swaths of blue light stacking into black.

—There was this old lady at the slots tonight, Linda says. I brought her a Screwdriver and told her the cherry was the same color as her lipstick, and she said, "That's great, sweetie," and tipped me a quarter.

—You ask for three more?

—Of course not.

—I would've.

—No, you wouldn't.

—You don't know that.

—Yes, I do.

Nolan pulls her closer, and she makes herself more comfortable against him. Her hair smells of shampoo and cigarette smoke.

—She must've sat there for three hours, just pulling the handle and nursing that Screwdriver. When I picked up her empty, you could see all the lines in her lips at the spot where she'd sipped from. But the crazy thing is, later, when I was taking this one jackass a Seabreeze, I saw it again. It was faint, you know, from the washer, but her lips were still there.

Dirtbag patted me on the tush when I took his order and then didn't even move to tip when I went to set it down. And I wanted to, I did, but instead I just said, "Oh, this one's dirty. I'll bring you a freshy."

Headlights, pulling into the complex of condominiums, wash over the back sides of the blinds and push long, skinny shadows across the bedroom walls in a slow collapse.

—That's a tough one, Nolan says, tracing the contours of her bare hip with his fingertips.

—I saw it at the bar, but I debated it the entire tray.

—You did the right thing.

—I didn't want his bad karma.

Nolan moves his fingers down and then up the curve of her spine.

—How's work? she says.

—Work's work.

Imitating Nolan's voice, she says:

—Work's work.

—What do you want me to say?

—Nothing you don't want to.

—I don't.

He brings his hand back to the hard protrusion of her hip and lets his fingers stand there before collapsing down to the heel of his palm. After a few seconds of quiet, he says:

—We're putting the finishing touches on that place I told you about.

—The McMansion?

—Yeah.

—How'd it turn out?

—Like a gold-plated turd.

She laughs.

—What's next?

—Move down the block three lots.

—Same floor plan?

—Bottom to top, but reversed.

—You looking for anything else?

—I don't know. Not yet.

Nolan stares at the ceiling, at bars of shadow, bars of light.

—Guy set himself on fire yesterday.

—What?

—A house painter.

—How'd he do that?

—Lit a cigarette when he shouldn't have.

—My God. Is he OK?

—He got burned pretty bad, and his back's busted from the fall, but he's alive.

—Were you there?

—I was.

—How awful.

—I didn't know him all that well. He usually comes on when we're finishing up.

—Still.

—Yeah.

—Is he married?

—He is.

—Kids?

—None that I know of.

—I didn't mean you, jerk.

—I didn't mean me—

—I'm joking.

—Oh.

—You're slow tonight.

—Sleepy.

—I stole all your chi.

—Is that what it is?

—More like too much beer. And whiskey, by the taste of it.

—Yeah, well, quit working nights.

—Are you going to make an honest woman out of me?

—I wouldn't put you through that.

—I wouldn't let you.

Then:

—She must be a wreck.

—She's holding up. I went and saw them at the hospital this morning.

—Can you imagine?

Nolan doesn't respond. He takes her hand in his own and he tries to feel the softness of her palm through his calluses. After a moment, Linda says:

—You're a good person. To visit her.

—Well, that goes without saying.

She swats Nolan's chest.

—You're awful.

To avoid confessing to the lie he's just told her, Nolan pulls her tightly against him and they remain like that for a few minutes without speaking until she says:

—You sleepy?

—Nope. You?

—Uh unh, she says, bringing herself up on him while biting her lower lip.

—Music to my ears.

He awakes in the dark just before dawn and walks lightly down the stairs to her kitchen where their clothes lie strewn across the linoleum. His pressed blue jeans and pearl-buttoned plaid lie in heaps on the floor, but his hat is crown down on the table where she'd placed it on her cashmere. He likes how she always makes something of them slowly undressing one another on the way to her bedroom. How they stop to kiss against Navajo-white walls. Cupping her naked ass pressed against the oil-based cool of the door jamb's trim.

He drinks directly from the sink faucet and the cool water collects on the side of his cheek before funneling down to the brushed stainless basin. The clock on the oven casts the room in a soft blue-green hue. Nolan shuts off the faucet, wipes his mouth on the back of his hand, and sits at a pine breakfast table with his elbow against a stack of dental hygiene textbooks. A receipt from the College of Southern Nevada bookmarks one of the texts. Nolan stretches his long legs out toward the sliding glass door that leads to her concrete patio slab. Above the fence boards on the patio, red and green airplane lights flash on their climb from McCarran. The plane disappears abruptly beyond the wall where the glass door ends.

As a boy, he wondered regularly for the better part of a year how the fire got down into the cooks' lungs, and when he finally got up the nerve to ask his father, he'd said that the chemicals they were using had gotten down in there, too, and that the fire had followed.

That something would behave so persistently troubled Nolan into his early adolescence, until he mentioned this to his mother one weekend morning on their drive home from the school library. She settled the matter firmly for him:

—It's not like the fire knew what it was doing, buddy. That's just how fire works.

Nolan turns his eyes from the kitchen wall to a hibachi

squatting at the center of the otherwise empty patio. One night, not too long back, he grilled spicy, marinated shrimp for Linda after she passed a test on the way to earning her Associates Degree in Dental Hygiene. They drank a bottle of rosé and made love on the kitchen counter, on the carpeted stairs leading up to her bedroom, at the foot of her bed. He woke up on the floor next to her, tangled in cotton sheets. He watched her snore, mouth open and head thrown back, the deep guttural snores of deep sleep. She'd never been dearer to him than in that moment, but why? When he shifted his weight, she closed her mouth and turned into him and he closed his eyes and fell back to sleep.

A street lamp shines on the hibachi. He can see finger marks on the lid, marks left in the grease, pollen, and dust residue, those made by his own hand, perhaps. Or made by some other man. No, he knows, no other man's hands but his own.

He sits there, just thinking about the painter and his wife, about the lie he told Linda, about the joke he made afterwards to disguise it. He can feel a part of himself becoming again the cad he's been before, the one who picks up and leaves a place to avoid that self, only to take it with him wherever he goes. It's easier for him to lie or to slip away from confrontations of this sort. He's come to be OK with being that kind of coward.

The refrigerator compressor switches on, electricity flowing through its copper veins. Soon, Nolan hears her footsteps on the stairs. Her ankle joint cracks when she hits the tiled landing. She comes to stand behind him and she wraps her arms around his shoulders and places her hands against his chest. She lays her cheek on the top of his head. He can feel the collar of her plush terrycloth robe against his shoulders. The robe she wears mornings when they have coffee together, sitting on her leather couch, her feet tucked up beneath her, listening to music on her laptop. She teases him for having never been on the Internet.

—What's wrong? she asks.

—Nothing. I just needed a sip of water.

—What were you thinking about?

—About how nice your jeans look on the floor like that.

—I'm serious.

—Me, too.

—I don't believe you.

—That's too bad, I mean it.

—I mean it, too.

Nolan reaches down and cups the slope of her calf, smooth in the palm of his callused hand.

—You're cold, he says.

—It's cold down here.

—Let's get you back to bed.

—No, tell me.

—I wasn't thinking anything important. Honest.

—You swear?

—I do.

—OK. I'll trust you.

The aluminum stairs that lead to the foreman's single-wide office clang under Nolan's boot steps. He raps on the hollow core door.

—It's open.

Inside, the foreman sits at his desk, hunched over the newspaper. He holds a small mixing bowl in one hand and a soup spoon in the other. He wears his reading glasses perched just below the bridge of his nose. The room smells of drip coffee and cigarette smoke, smells Nolan has come to associate with the foreman. Nolan removes his work hat as he enters the office.

—Coffee? the foreman offers.

—I'm all right, thanks.

The foreman holds up the bowl.

—Rabbit pellets?

—I'll pass.

Lifting the empty bowl toward Nolan, he says:

—Bran cereal and banana slices, Jackson. This is what becomes of married men. Remember that.

—Yes, sir.

The foreman sets the bowl on the newspaper and drops in the spoon. He leans back in his chair and reaches into the pocket of his work shirt for the soft pack of generic menthols he keeps there.

—What can I do you for?

Nolan looks at the scarred linoleum and scratches an itch at his temple with a hooked right forefinger.

—I was hoping I might draw early, for the past week.

The foreman lights his cigarette, sets the lighter on the desk, and sits back comfortably.

—You need me to advance you for the whole two?

—No, sir, just what I'm owed.

Nolan meets the foreman's eyes through the smoke and something in them makes him look down at where his hands finger his hat brim.

—Moving on down the line? the foreman asks.

—Yes, sir.

The foreman sighs smoke. His desk is cluttered with blueprints and carpenter pencil stubs, cheap ball points bearing advertisements for real-estate agencies and tool makers. An array of business cards have been taped or tacked to the cork board hanging against the particle-board paneling over his shoulder. In an upper corner of the rectangular board, the 23rd Infantry Division shoulder-sleeve insignia, four white stars on a shield of blue felt. He looks Nolan over judiciously.

—How about a raise?

—That's awfully kind, but—

—How about a raise, a twelver of watery domestic, and a lap dance over at the Gulch every other Friday night?

—Like a gift certificate sort of thing?

—Hell, no. Cash money. I'll even chaperone and spend most of it on myself.

Nolan looks down at his hat and smiles.

—That's a generous offer, but—

—Bet your ass it is. Twelver alone would keep me on this detail. Gulch is just icing on the cake.

—Yes, sir.

—But you're antsy to move on.

—Yes, sir.

—Any chance you'll be back?

—I doubt that.

—Well, I hate to lose you, lost as you get in that head of yours.

—Thank you, sir.

—That wasn't a compliment. He smiles.

—No, sir, Nolan grins.

—I'll talk with the girl when she gets in. She'll get things squared away.

—I appreciate it.

Nolan steps forward and extends his hand across the foreman's desk. The foreman stands and they shake.

—I figured I'd work out the day.

—Don't be doing us any favors, now.

—No, I'd planned on it.

—All right, then.

Nolan turns, and the foreman lowers himself into his seat, but just as Nolan reaches the door, the foreman says:

—Old butthead's wife said she enjoyed your visit at the hospital the other day. Said you had nothing but nice things to say about him.

Nolan looks down at the door knob. Brushed stainless. Same as Linda's sink.

—Didn't think I'd mention it?

Nolan turns to face the foreman.

—I thought you might.

—You're not thinking it's your fault or some stupid nonsense like that, are you?

—No, sir, that ain't it.

—Good. My wife pulls that crap. Drives me nuts.

—I just didn't know what to say.

—There wasn't nothing to say. I mean, look, I don't mean to lecture you, but something like this, you were there, you witnessed it, and that means you show up, look his wife in the eye, and mumble something about how sorry you are that she married a stupid, clumsy man, and you hope they never breed if he can ever get it up again long enough to try.

—Yes, sir.

—After that, you just stand around for at least fifteen minutes making small talk, sipping burnt, rotgut coffee, and praying to God that some well-endowed nurse comes in demanding to take your temperature.

Nolan looks down at his hands.

—Yes, sir.

—Most times, the foreman says, it ain't knowing what to say as much as it is just being there not knowing how to say it.

—I know.

—I hope so, Jackson. I really do.

2

He descends into Death Valley at dawn by way of Daylight Pass, the shadows of his truck and Airstream trailer passing systematically over the desert landscape. His profile, distinct and familiar, glides over a blur of wildflower, rock, and sand. Beyond the dusty windshield, thirteen westbound contrails converge above the Panamint Range, the uppermost peaks of which still bear a light dusting of snow.

The morning is bright and cold and the landscape vast and desolate until the headlights of an oncoming vehicle catch Nolan's attention. Using the ends of his fingers, he steers the Ranger and trailer back into his own lane. He steadies his hands on the wheel, gauges his parameters, and the vehicles pass without incident.

He glances over at his profile, rushing across the earth. Bright sunlight surrounding the shadow-shape of his features and his Western hat, his arms up and his hands on the wheel. He likes how he appears, all velocity and direction. He starts to reach up to touch the brim of his hat in a lighthearted salute, but thought of Linda and the painter's wife and people like them stops him. He turns from his profile, and his shadow follows suit, as if it had any choice in matter.

At Zabriskie Point Nolan quits the road to stretch his legs and to admire the hoodoo badlands. Shadows drape the jagged spines of the erosions and cling to the steep sides of the narrow canyons. He walks the asphalt path to the elevated panorama. He studies three metal placards stationed before the vista to explain the geology and the history of the place. Then he sits on the low rock wall bordering the overlook and vista. He runs his hands over the sun-warmed rocks while admiring the construction of the wall. He considers the hands that placed each rock.

Before him, horizontal bands of tawny and red run almost perpendicular to slender upthrusts of brown and black. Nolan traces rills and gullies with his eyes, follows the flow down deep gulches and along distant waterlines of an ancient lake. To the north, Manly Beacon, shaped by desert downpours. A range of consistencies set before him, stages and methods of erosion. Someplace in the gradual upheaval and sink, fossilized animal tracks and grasses and reeds that once swayed beneath the same sun. Other than the grainy stirrings of a low wind, the quiet of the badlands is immense, the sunlight blinding.

He's not there for more than ten minutes when a tri-axle tour bus lumbers around a bend in the highway and parks in the turnout beside his truck and Airstream. Side mirrors extend from either side of the bulging windshield like insect antennae. The waxed exterior of the coach gleams in the sunlight. After the engine settles to idle, the door to the bus opens with a hydraulic wheeze and a spit of dust. Two dozen retirees disembark, chattering like grackle. The men wear short-sleeve, button-up shirts tucked into khakis and the women wear sunhats. They all wear sunglasses and most of them carry disposable plastic bottles of water. They walk slowly up the pathway to the promontory, the line stretching and thinning, a pilgrims' procession.

As the tourists spread out along the wall or gather around the placards, one woman breaks off from the group and walks directly over to where Nolan sits alone on the rock wall. She takes a seat less than an arm's length away from him, and says:

—Phew.

—You made it.

—Plenty more where that came from, sonny.

—No doubt, ma'am. No doubt.

From her purse, the woman produces a soft pack of 100s and peels back the foil. She gives the pack a seasoned shake and offers one of the protruding cigarettes to Nolan.

—Coffin nail?

—I'm all right, thanks.

—Suit yourself.

The woman lights a cigarette and exhales. Then, she passes the slender wand over the view before them.

—Spectacular vista, she says as blue tendrils of smoke dissipate in the wake of her slow-moving hand.

—Yes, ma'am.

—Where I'm from, Orlando, it's all flat. Only way to get above sea level is to drive an overpass.

—Sounds pretty flat.

—Very flat. Nothing pretty about it.

The woman makes a fist with her cigarette hand and jerks her thumb over her shoulder in the direction of Nolan's Airstream, glaring in the morning sunlight.

—My third husband had one of those. Begged me on his deathbed to bury him in it. You know what a hole like that would cost to dig?

—It'd have to be some hole.

—Decided to take myself on vacation instead.

The woman brings the cigarette to her mouth to conceal her smile and smoke collects beneath the brim of her sunhat. A second or two later, she says:

—That was a joke.

—Yes, ma'am.

They sit quietly. The day is already warm and the woman smells pleasantly of sunblock and tobacco smoke. Nolan watches a group of men, standing at the placards, point to the illustrations and then up to the mountains in the distance, immediate and far.

—Are you going to tell me where you're from, cowboy, or are you going to make an old lady ask?

—No, ma'am.

—No, you're not going to tell me, or, no, you're not going to make me ask?

Nolan smiles and shakes his head. The woman also smiles.

—Truth is, ma'am, it's been a long time since I've been from one place in particular.

—So you're a bum.

—No, ma'am. I ain't no bum.

—What, then? A drifter?

—I'm a journeyman carpenter, ma'am.

The woman brings the cigarette to her mouth, presses it between the furrows in her lips, and inhales deeply.

—Are you looking for work out here?

—This here's beyond my skill set.

The woman smiles at this, and her teeth reveal weathered ridges similar to those beyond where they sit, similar save for a difference in scale.

—So, what then? Sit here and wait until something comes up?

—No, ma'am, I'm just passing through.

—Where to?

Nolan hesitates before answering.

—It's been a long time since I've seen the ocean.

—How old are you?

—Creeping up on thirty-two.

She shakes her head.

—Must be nice.

Then:

—My grandson's thirty-two. Flies a drone for the Air Force. His body's here, but his mind's over there. How this works, I'm too old to understand.

Nolan looks down at his hands and nods.

—At Thanksgiving this year, his wife said he's the only man who comes home from war smelling of deodorant sweat. Better that than mustard gas, I told her.

The woman shakes her head. In a tone of conciliation, she says:

—Before her time.

She brings the cigarette back to her mouth and for a moment she and Nolan sit without speaking while the other tourists mill about, taking pictures and applying sunblock, or sharing time at the placards. The sounds of laughs and voices and movements echo weakly over the badlands. Finally, the woman says:

—Have you ever seen satellite photos of Earth at night?

—You mean from outer space?

—Yes, outer space. What're you, suddenly slow?

—No, ma'am.

—You sure about that?

—Hopefully.

—I don't understand how this fills you with hope? Do you mean to say, I hope not?

Nolan looks up from the heel of his boot and directly into the woman's face for the first time.

—You don't let up, do you? He smiles.

She lowers her sunglasses and stares intently at him through fragile, light green eyes. She points the end of her cigarette at him, three-quarters of an inch of ash waiting to break off between them.

—The words you speak, she says.

—And the company you keep, he finishes.

The woman winks at Nolan and then raises the sunglasses over her eyes and turns to the view. Staring ahead, she says:

—Two words describe what Earth looks like at night from outer space.

—All right.

—Lava flow.

He boondocks early that evening in a pull-through slot at the North Star Mobile Park just outside Independence, California, on Highway 395. He sits inside his Airstream, at the small Formica table at the front of the trailer, patiently worrying a jumble of eight-penny galvanized nails in the palm of his hand. The door is open to the last of the daylight. Canned laughter from a syndicated sitcom reaches him from the television inside a neighboring double-wide, the wheels removed from its axles and a green plastic apron wrapped around its waist.

A warm breeze slips through the trailer's screened door smelling faintly of propane. The breeze lifts the corner of a calendar pinned to a kitchen cabinet Nolan made from redwood lath boards he salvaged from a remodel in Reno, Nevada. One side of the cabinet bears the pencil drawing of a swan he found on the board after yanking free wallpaper and plaster. Beneath the swan is the year 1905. The breeze also lifts the edge of the road atlas spread out on the table before Nolan. It lifts the edge of the two-page letter he's just written to Linda, a neat version of the rough draft he spent most the day composing in his mind and on a yellow legal pad.

With the nails cupped in his left hand, Nolan rests the length of his forearm on the table and uses the palm and fingers of his hand to manipulate the jumble so as to free one nail at a time, as if he were preparing to hammer up siding or down subfloor. Staring vacantly at the network of lines on the atlas, Nolan sets a freed nail on the letter and begins unjumbling the next one. It's a form of meditation, untangling nails, something he gleaned from an old timer he watched practice it at lunch each day on the site where they both labored as rough framers.

—This is what we used to do before nail guns, the old timer told Nolan when the young journeyman asked him what he was doing. This was before all the *pop-pop-pop* you young bucks got nowdays.

The man would sit in the shade and eat his lunch and untangle nails, mindlessly, it seemed, extricating one at a time from the sharp confusion.

Nolan sets another nail on the handwritten letter. The scent of singed hair lingers at the back of his throat. The colorful nips of wire-stripping clinging to the burns on the painter's face. The awkward bend of his neck.

From the television next door sounds the indecipherable speech of actors in a television sitcom.

When the last of the nails is arranged before him, Nolan stands and walks over to the cabinet and tucks the corner of the calendar behind its tab. Above the grid of days and dates, a glossy photograph of cold ocean waves crashing over wet black rocks. A redwood-lined crag in the distance. *The Lost Coast* written in tiny letters at the bottom right corner. Nolan leans against the cabinet, feeling the warm breeze on his forearms, the sleeves of his shirt rolled up and in.

He looks down at the letter, and in the shadows falling across it he remembers light ripples from the community pool playing up the side of Linda's condominium the first night he knocked on her door. Vacillating shadows and waves of artificial light fluttering up the T-111 siding, over the latex-painted eaves, and into the night, gone.

At the back of his trailer his work hat and his dress hat lie crown down in the arms of a Western hat hanger. Below this, the oak dresser in which Nolan keeps the few clothes he owns. He traded for the dresser at a flea market in Phoenix, Arizona, refurbished it himself and adorned each drawer with a pair of stamped-brass, winged-hourglass pulls he'd come across in Truth or Consequences, New Mexico. Mounted above his bed is a long, rectangular bookshelf made of stained barn wood that he salvaged in Ashton, Idaho, and stocked over time with carefully chosen field guides, road atlases of the western United States, and a small collection of used paperbacks, each one read several times through. For his wash space, a lead mirror hangs above a brushed stainless oval sink he bartered for in Eden, Wyoming. The mirror is set in a rectangular frame he crafted from quarter-sawn oak and is held fast by mortise and tenon, the chamfered ends of which stand a little proud. His kitchen sink is cast iron and porcelain. Its bronze faucet found in broad daylight on a sidewalk in Sparks, Nevada. The countertop is soapstone, gifted to him in Eureka, California. Alongside the trailer's only door, a barometer, thermometer, and compass, and adjacent to these, a walnut curio box displays several handsome arrowheads and old coins, a rusted railroad spike, a long, slender piece of river-smoothed brick, a chunk of asphalt he came across in a forest near no road, and a bird's nest constructed from lace lichen and wild oat stalks, boar hair and a broken toothpick still wrapped in its cellophane sleeve.

He was nineteen years old when he bought the trailer. Gutted it that very same day. Thirteen years later and it's still a work in progress. He looks at the hats, carefully placed to preserve their shape. He knows what the hats signify and he knows how he feels when he's wearing them, with his eyes shaded and his line of sight obscured from others. He wasn't raised among men who wear Western hats, but he's come to feel most at ease around them.

He sits comfortably surrounded by his possessions. He knows they travel well and can be readily found when needed, for he's arranged his belongings carefully. For nearly half his life Nolan's worked to fashion order in the world. He's cut and joined rock, metal, plastic, wire, and wood, and still mastery eludes him. Still it wills away, and what he works something into, chance and time undo elegantly and infinitely, beyond his ken of patience and perception, everything new commencing toward unravel and decay.

Outside, the breeze gains some, and the pages of the atlas and the letter struggle against the weight of the electroplated nails, coated in zinc oxide to fortify them against corrosion and rust. Canned laughter sounds from the adjacent double-wide, canned laughter and applause and the jingle that leads the audience to a commercial break.

3

Noon the next day Nolan navigates the Kingsbury Grade, switchbacks carved into the eastern face of the Sierra Nevada, a granite tsunami cresting over basin and range. Small mansions dot the lower portion of the escarpment, and the sun shines yellow white in their picture windows. He takes the switchbacks in low gear, up through impressive road cuts and past wind-twisted pine while keeping to paths made by previous travelers and concentrating on the sounds his tires make on the sanded roadway. The shadows of his Ranger and Airstream drift over the last of the snow fields, still glittering beyond the splattered road banks.

In South Shore, just across the California state line at Lake Tahoe, Nolan stops at a gas station to shave in the men's room. Gang graffiti and unaffiliated handstyles adorn the walls and the saccharine stink of urinal cake suffuses the tiny bathroom. Above the bathroom mirror, someone has written on the wall:

It's only the world. Let it burn.

Nolan warms the razor in a steady column of hot water and then draws his face from behind a mask of soap. He taps the razor on the edge of the sink, knocking free clumpy shards of wet hair along the porcelain bowl. With the water steaming the bathroom mirror and his face half-shaved, he lowers the razor and stands there, gathering the words on the wall in the wool of his mind.

A little over an hour later, he quits Interstate 50 west of Placerville and cuts out for a back road that leads into the foothills of El Dorado County. The lush, green hillsides are easy on his eyes after all his time in the desert. Craggy oaks stand leafless and black against the grasses, and clusters of mistletoe ball in the upper reaches of the bare canopy. The road follows the contours of the rolling landscape, landscape he surveys with the knowledge of someone who once knew it well.

Before long, he turns right on a gravel road that leads a quarter mile downhill to a ranch house surrounded by tall oaks. He stops the truck before the house, kills the engine, and listens to it tink and cool. Smoke drifts from the chimney, low over the composite roofing, down into the lasts of a well-tended winter garden and among the starts already planted for spring and summer. A cat slinks around a neatly stacked woodpile, meticulously covered with a blue tarp and lashed fast with bungee cords. An older model Accord, kept up, is parked in front of the garage. Nolan pushes back the brim of his hat with his thumb and smells the wood smoke on cold air filling the cab. He is sitting there, looking over the basin of a long, west-facing slope, when the front door opens and his mother steps out drying her hands on a cotton dishtowel. She shakes her head and smiles. Before opening the cab door, he reaches across the bench seat for a bouquet of carnations he bought at the gas station in South Shore.

★

He stands with his back to the fireplace as he admires an oak banquet table his father crafted from planks milled from a tree that fell on the property during a winter rain storm when Nolan was fifteen. The table is almost completely hidden by antiques and collectibles, items that fill the small living room: ornate chairs and metal children's toys; book cases housing bronze bookends and pewter flasks; galvanized tubs filled with old tools; brass weathervanes leaning against a leather-covered trunk filled with vases of cameo glass wrapped in newspaper; stacks of old popular magazines; World War I gas masks; World War II fighter-pilot gear; an upright piano; collections of Zippo lighters, medicine bottles, ceramic mugs, arrowheads, china dish sets, campaign buttons, brass compasses, polished silverware; a cluttered assortment of beads and pins and old coins; all this and more.

Nolan's mother weaves her way into the living room from the kitchen carrying a mug of hot black coffee and a buttered piece of toasted banana nut bread.

—Here you go, she says, handing Nolan the mug and toast.

—Thank you.

—My pleasure.

Nolan takes a bite of the homemade bread and washes it down with a sip of the coffee.

—Better than ever, he says.

—It's gluten free.

—I don't know what that means.

—It means all those years of stomachaches and inflammation your father used to complain about wasn't my cooking.

—He didn't mean—

—I'm joking, Nolan. It means there's not much wheat in my diet anymore. Doctor's orders.

—Everything all right?

—Everything's fine. She said, change my diet or take a pill.

—She really offer you a pill?

—No, she was joking. But she said there is one.

—Of course there is.

—She said you can buy just about anything from Canada these days.

—I believe it.

—Your Aunt Grace said Uncle John orders boxfuls of those little blue pills for a fraction of the price.

Nolan tries to hide his smile behind the coffee mug.

—Boxfuls?

His mother smiles.

—They've always been very active.

Nolan nods. Lowering the mug, he says:

—This lady doctor the one who took over for Dr Shepherd?

—Yes.

—Sounds like she's a good fit for you.

—Dr Shepherd was a good man, but it makes a world of difference for a woman to be able to go to a woman doctor for woman things.

—I never thought of that.

—Why would you?

Nolan lowers his eyes to the coffee.

—This is delicious, he says.

—I'm glad I had some on hand for you.

She returns to the kitchen and stirs chicken stock simmering on the gas range. Leafy green remnants litter an antique butcher's block at the center of the kitchen. A collection of postcards that Nolan has sent to his mother from his travels over the years are held fast by magnets to the side of the refrigerator. He walks among the antiques, scrupulously placed about the room.

—Lot of new pieces here, Mom.

—God bless the Internet.

—That right?

—Just the other day I sold a seasoning rack for ninety dollars.

Nolan whistles a short note while his mother walks over to the sink and begins filling a tall drinking glass from the faucet.

—Guess where to, she says.

—China.

—How'd you know?

—Lucky guess.

When the glass is full, she carries it over to where a writing desk stands beside a white bed sheet that has been pinned halfway up the wall. The sheet hangs down over a stool, the backdrop to the photos she takes of items she posts for sale on the web to supplement her income.

—Come here, she says to Nolan. I want you to see something.

Alongside the desk a large clear-plastic bag sits slumped full of packaging material.

—This is so neat, she says.

Nolan's mother picks out a single piece of the packaging material and holds it up for his inspection. Then, she drops it in the glass of water and the piece dissolves immediately.

—Rice, she says, grinning with satisfaction.

—Whatever happened to good old-fashioned Styrofoam?

—Frank thinks that one day, millions of years from now, some species will mine Styrofoam the way we do diamonds.

—Who's Frank? Nolan tilts his head, smiling, but his

mother sets the glass on the table and turns back toward the kitchen.

—A friend.

—Do I get to meet him?

—Not yet.

Raising the mug to his mouth, Nolan says:

—Yet is good.

—We'll see.

His mother returns to the chopping block and picks up the knife.

—What does Frank do for a living? Nolan goads playfully.

—Very funny.

—He at least drinking age?

—Not funny.

—Where'd you two meet?

—He's the new principal.

—What happened to Ms Baker?

—A group of Evangelicals scared up a witch hunt.

—So, now you're dating your boss? Nolan's grin growing.

—As the school librarian, he's only marginally my boss.

—That's one way to look at it.

—Are you finished?

—Is he a nice man?

His mother stops chopping and sets the knife on the block with her hand still on the handle, her knuckles down on the smoothed wood. Without turning her head to him, she responds:

—In the way I want a man to be, yes, he is.

—Good.

Nolan watches the remnants of the packaging material settle to the bottom of the glass.

—How're the kids? he asks, moving on.

—It seems like the girls wear less and less each day and fewer and fewer of the boys know how to read.

—You think there's a correlation there?

—Is the Pope Catholic?

—This where you side with the Evangelicals?

—Sometimes I think things have gotten to the point where I don't know where I side. Like it's all just confusion and complexity.

—I know what you mean.

—There's always been division. Bitter division. But there used to be more compromise. Now, compromise is weak.

His mother resumes chopping. She says:

—A while back, the governor said something along the lines of, crush your enemies and drive them before you.

—I read about that.

—But Frank told me he was quoting some movie he was in.

—I read that, too.

—I mean, what kind of reality are we living in?

—California.

—I guess.

Nolan carries his mug of coffee over to the fireplace mantle, made from the same wood as the banquet table, another of his father's pieces. Framed photographs on the mantle show a young Nolan standing alongside his Airstream. Next to this, a photo of Nolan's brother, Chance, sitting beside their father on a river bank, the both of them fishing, their father with a cigarette at the corner of his smile. Nolan's smile.

—Tell me what you've been building, his mother says from the kitchen.

—Same old, same old.

—Monster tract homes?

—Customer's always right.

—The amount of energy it must take to keep one of those things going.

—Amount of energy it takes to build one.

—You'd think that by 2007 we'd have some things figured out. I just don't get it.

—Not much to get.

—I guess not, she says. Did you like living in Las Vegas?

—I didn't dislike it.

—What happened to Arizona? You liked Arizona.

—I got tired of working nights, building under those flood lamps. That's no way to do carpentry.

—I read somewhere that fifteen of the world's twenty largest hotels are in Vegas.

—I watched them demolish the Stardust.

—Did you?

—They had water sprinklers out to try and keep down the dust, but people just ended up running like mad from the clouds. I hear you can watch it on the Internet.

—Did you go see the Hoover Dam?

—They searched my truck before I drove over it.

—Why?

—I could've been a terrorist.

—My generation experienced life much differently than yours.

—Usually the case.

—This seems different, though.

—Is what it is.

—I've never liked that saying. It's too easy.

—Nature takes the path of least resistance.

—You think all this is natural?

—You sound like Dad.

—Where do you think he stole his good ideas from?

—Oh, he always gave you credit.

—Later, he did.

—Just his way of teasing.

—Odd way of teasing.

Alongside the photograph of Nolan's brother and father, a Purple Heart and a Bronze Star, both framed. Nolan reaches up and checks the frames for dust with the ends of his fingers and finds none.

—Is there a special lady in your life? his mother asks from the kitchen.

—I was seeing a woman down in Vegas, but we were headed in different directions.

—You mean you left town.

Nolan doesn't respond.

—Do you know where you're headed next?

—It's been a long time since I've seen the ocean.

—Any place in particular?

—I haven't decided yet.

Then, he says:

—When'd you bring out Dad's medals?

—I don't know, some time ago.

Next to the medals, a picture of Nolan's parents on their wedding day. Standing on the steps of City Hall, his mother in a white dress and his father in suit and tie. The sun in their eyes.

His father was a scion of east-coast industrialists. The wayward son. His mother's baby and his father's foil. The headstrong child who rebelled by lashing himself first to counterculture ideals and then further by volunteering for service in Vietnam. There, he came to acknowledge the privileges he had, but had conveniently ignored during what his father called his pro-longed adolescence. He served one tour, during which his mother passed away. The paper of the letter his sister wrote softened by the humidity of the jungle. He came home humbled, to find his father senile and bitter and his brothers positioning themselves around the family fortune. He left it all behind and hitchhiked to California, where he slept on the beaches and yo-yoed up and down the coastline before swinging inland to follow the paths of Muir, Harte, and Twain.

Nolan studies his parents' faces, their smiles and their eyes. Complex souls full of contradictions.

His mother was pregnant with Chance, but not noticeably, when the wedding-day photo was taken. She was a native northern California daughter who left Placerville for UC Berkeley at seventeen and returned, quietly proud, four years later to work as an elementary-school librarian, a sharp, kind wit whom grown students would return to visit through the years to thank her for helping them to become lifelong readers.

She was first in her family to go to college, and one of only a few women in the town to do so. On her return after graduation, while walking beneath the weathered dummy hanging from the Hangman's Tree on Main Street, she realized how conflicted she felt toward her hometown, not only about the place's history, but toward the townspeople, who came to view her with suspicion. They were envious and distrustful of her education, she felt, scornful of a woman with an education. Her older brothers had gone into the trades and her younger sister had gotten pregnant in high school. Her mother and father both had tears in their eyes when the three of them gathered to hang her degree on the living-room wall, handsomely framed and prominently placed. The animosity that piece of paper generated from her own siblings and her community she transformed within herself into a point of quiet pride.

Nolan looks at his father. He wonders if the suit is the same one they buried him in. It couldn't be, could it? He'd only seen him wear a suit to weddings and to funerals and it was always the same one. Normally, he wore denim and leather. The Texas tuxedo, Nolan would hear it called. At work, he wore canvas coveralls. His name embroidered on a patch ironed over his heart.

His parents met in the summer of 1972 at Placerville Hardware, the oldest continually operating hardware store west of the Mississippi. Their father was buying a gold pan, and a tarp to shade the campsite he'd staked out on the American River. He wasn't doing much then other than reading philosophy and playing a five-string guitar. Their mother was in the store to buy an extension cord.

—I smelled him before I saw him, she liked to joke.

He asked her name and she looked him up and down and asked him how old he was. He smiled and told her and next she asked him if he had a job.

—And then he got all smart and asked why, and I told him I had no interest in dating a man I would have to support. So, he walked right up to the counter at the hardware store and asked if they were hiring. A week later he was renting a room across from the Gold Bug and we were picnicking down on the river.

Her pregnancy wasn't a secret. Her siblings were only too happy to see her finally do something her parents didn't approve of. She told Nolan on one of his visits home after his father's death that she knew she'd broken their hearts, despite their standing by her and never saying she had.

—Good people, she often called them.

Nolan reads the details of the photograph. He sees in it all he knows and doesn't know of his family's history.

—I always wanted to see the Hoover Dam, his mother says to him from the kitchen. Your father used to say it's something worth seeing.

—It is, Nolan says, reaching up to turn the picture's frame slightly.

—You think you'll head back to Vegas after seeing the ocean?

—I doubt it.

The next morning, Nolan unhitches the Airstream and drives his Ranger to the supermarket, where he purchases a single daffodil bulb in full bloom. At Placerville Union he removes his hat and squats beside his father's grave and, using the claw of his hammer, digs a small hole and plants the daffodil just above the granite marker. The bulbs from his previous visits are also in bloom. He digs quietly beneath the late April sky, ragged with clouds, and when he finishes, he takes his hat in his hands but he remains squatting beside the marker.

Uphill, seven soldiers in dress uniforms loiter beneath a collapsible aluminum and plastic tent. Men younger than Nolan, who lounge in the empty rows of white folding chairs arranged for a ceremony still some time off. Their polished helmets set on the seats of the chairs, their rifles leaning against the seat backs. To the side of the chairs, hidden behind flower wreaths and a poster board decorated with photographs, or photocopies of them, artificial turf partially conceals a mound of dirt. Parked beyond this, a backhoe, blatant yellow in an otherwise green and gray setting.

Nolan pulls a dandelion from the side of his father's marker and specks of dirt scatter over it and into the lines of the dead man's name:

CHANCE NOLAN JACKSON
1947–1996
Loving Husband and Father
Veteran of the War in Vietnam

Nolan was twenty years old and rolling trusses in the cool of night under stadium lights in the desert of New Mexico when his father passed on. The foreman handed him a folded slip of paper from the office that said he needed to call home. He left New Mexico before dawn the next day.

The wind stirs a dogwood downhill. Nolan watches the wind rattle the pink petals, watches it bend the daffodils on their slender stalks. He brushes dirt from his father's granite marker. He traces the laser-carved letters of his name. His own name. A decision Nolan despised his father for during his adolescence and loved him for more intensely after his death. Chance, too. But Chance so much so that when he turned eighteen and left for Berkeley, he changed his name to Cosmo Swift.

—Whatever the fuck that means, Nolan remembers his father saying with a hint of pride for his son's determination to break free of the father.

In the end, though, it was Chance who returned home and Nolan who broke free. Chance changed his name but

Nolan drove distance between them. In the handful of times he stopped home before his father's death, he sensed that his father's pride had shifted. Chance's break was symbolic. It was words. But Nolan constructed something new of himself. If ever he felt a desire to return, this small happiness he saw in his father kept him further away.

Nolan stands and puts on his hat. One of the soldiers walks out from beneath the tent and tosses his helmet in the air. As Nolan walks to his truck, he watches the young soldier toss and catch the polished chrome helmet. Despite the clouds and dull light, the helmet gleams.

That night, he carries two bottles of beer into the living room. His mother is sitting on the couch before the fire in the fireplace and he hands one of the bottles to her.

—Thanks for cleaning up, she says, accepting the beer.

—Least I could do.

Settling in beside her on the couch, he says:

—You had other plans for tonight, didn't you?

—I'm glad you're here.

—I should have called first.

—I'd still change plans to sit here with you.

—Yeah.

—It's been too long.

Nolan nods.

—Almost a year, he says.

—Shame on you.

—I know.

She pats Nolan on the knee. The ranch home stands quiet around them as firelight plays over the different surfaces of the antiques in the room.

—I went and saw Dad today.

—I figured you might. How is he?

—Still there.

—Far as we can tell.

Nolan shakes his head, smiling. His mother raises the bottle to her own smile.

—Bunch of soldiers were there, waiting on a funeral.

—A boy died in Iraq. It's been in the papers.

Nolan stretches his legs out comfortably before him, the toes of his clean white socks threaded with gold.

—I worked alongside this one guy, on a framing crew out in Idaho, he joined up after 9/11. I often wonder what happened to him.

—I thank God every night for the Marines not taking Chance. I know it hurt his pride, but I'm grateful for it.

Nolan scratches at the stubble on his jaw. He covers his mouth with his hand.

—What's on your mind? his mother asks.

—I regret, sometimes, not going.

—Don't talk nonsense.

—I mean it. I feel like sometimes the one thing I could have done in my life to make a difference came and went.

—Even with everything we know now?

—I mean Afghanistan.

—The Good War.

—You can't understand.

—Excuse me?

—I don't mean that to be harsh, Mom, but it's a fact.

—The need to experience war?

—To fight for something like that, yeah. Some men feel that.

—And you don't think women do?

—I think it's different.

—Which doesn't mean I can't understand it.

Slender flames sway and strike at oak rounds in the fireplace. With the damp bottom of the beer bottle, Nolan makes slow, wide circles around his kneecap, the movement leaving a wet mark in the blue of his jeans.

—Even with everything your father went through, you still feel that need?

—Those experiences made him who he was.

—A broken man.

—He wasn't broken.

—Maybe not for his sons he wasn't.

She looks down into the mouth of the bottle in her lap.

—Let me ask you something, she says. How long are you going to keep doing this?

—Thinking about the war?

—That will never go away. I'm talking about the roaming.

Nolan can feel the warmth of the fire against the back of his hand. The comfort and luxury of the moment, of a safe home. He watches the mark on his jeans dry and fade.

—I don't know.

—Don't you want a family?

—Sometimes I think about that, sure.

Raising her hand, palm up, ushering him gently:

—And what do you think?

—I don't know if I could bring someone into all of this.

—Bringing them in is the fun part.

Nolan smiles.

—I walked into that one.

Outside, the wind gains some, and moments later the flames of the fire, as if charmed, move with it. His mother sighs:

—No, she says, it's bringing them through that's the hard part.

—I don't know that I'd be any good at it.

—No one does. But it doesn't stop us.

—No.

—Biological imperative.

—You sound like Chance.

—He sounds like me.

—No, he sounds like Chance.

—Yes, he does.

Nolan tilts his bottle to measure its contents.

—Your father wouldn't have wanted you to join. He would have been furious to know that Chance got as far as taking the physical.

—He wanted to keep those experiences for himself.

—That's not it.

—He could be a selfish man.

—Says the son who hasn't seen his mother in almost a year.

—You know I can't live here.

—No, I don't. You've never explained this wanderlust of yours.

—There's too much of him here. Too much of me not being here when he was sick.

—There wasn't anything you could have done for him.

—I could have been here more.

—He liked that you were out there, exploring. My god, he loved your postcards. He would just lie in bed and look at them at night.

Nolan looks down at his hands.

—The place he made for me isn't the place I want.

—What does that mean?

—I feel trapped by all this.

—All what?

—The world.

—Now, you sound like Chance.

—It's like he set up this idea, when we were kids, that the world was a certain way, and I saw it that way—

—Because that's how he described it to you—

—And that's the problem. That's the way he described it, but that's not how I found it to be.

—You act like he was alone in it.

—I didn't really ever know Grandpa.

—I mean me. Your mother.

—You were always more realistic.

—Less broken.

Nolan stares into the fire.

—Yeah, he says, I guess so.

—When was the last time you spoke with your brother? his mother asks.

—It's been a while.

—Did you know that Dawn left him?

—No, I didn't.

—Seven months ago. He's boxed most everything up and moved all their furniture into the garage. When I was last out there, he spent all night playing video games or in his room writing. I got the feeling he's barely keeping his job at the newspaper, and I don't know this for certain, but I think it's only a matter of time before he loses the house.

She raises the bottle, but before sipping from it, she says:

—Ridiculous investment.

—What'd they pay?

—Six-fifty.

—That house isn't worth barely half that.

—California, his mother states.

—Not just California.

Nolan looks up at the photographs of his family arranged on the mantle. Photographs and his father's medals, the only obvious evidence in the room of his war. Evidence of his father's war, evidence of his grandfather's war in the room around him. Firelight dances across the photos, turning the shadows glossy. Nolan wonders what objects will become the antiques of his and Chance's war.

—Promise me something, he says then.

—What's that?

—No matter what happens between you and Frank—

—Nolan—

—Hear me out.

—We've been on a couple dates.

—And I'm glad for that.

—I think—

—Please. Hear me out.

—OK.

—Don't take down the photos of him. The medals.

—I wouldn't.

—I could see how another man might not like having to be around that—

—Frank's not that way—

—But if he turns out to be—

—Then, I'd never let it get that far.

She pats him on the knee.

—You remember the last time you were here with Chance?

—Right after Dad passed.

—You remember what he said about them? Our pictures?

—No.

—He stood right there and he said, "Someday, these will mean nothing to anyone."

—Always did have a way with words.

His mother smiles.

—Be nice.

—Not the nicest thing to say.

—No, but he's wrong. Look around you. All this stuff, my hobby, this stuff means something to me. It hasn't always been mine, and it won't be, but for the time that it is, I appreciate it.

—I'm not sure I see what that has to do with our pictures.

—What I'm trying to say is that you're a carpenter, Nolan, not a soldier. You're a builder, not a destroyer.

—Dad wasn't a destroyer.

—Yes, he was. In his own way, he was.

—What you're saying is, find a place and settle down.

—I'm saying give it a chance.

Wind swirls against the house and down the flue, fluttering the fire.

—What's Chance writing? Nolan asks after a moment passes.

—Something about Russian sailors.

—What the hell does he know about Russian sailors?

—He smokes a lot of marijuana these days. For his migraines.

Nolan shakes his head. Outside, the cat meows beneath the front door.

—I'm happy that you've gone and seen and done like you have, Nolan, I really am, even though I worry about you not settling down.

She hesitates.

—I don't think I've asked you for much since he passed, but I'd appreciate it if you'd check on Chance for me. Spend a night or two with him. Just check in on your way to the ocean.

—People's hearts get broken, Mom. Doesn't mean you get a free pass to be a stoner.

—There's something else at work, Nolan. Something's upsetting him. He writes me these rambling letters about the president this and Western civilization that. In the last one all he could talk about was "irrational exuberance." I sometimes daydream that a bunch of television people are camped in the front yard because Chance's been making bombs in his garage or gone into a post office with a loaded gun or something, and I don't know what to say to them. I don't know how to explain what I did wrong because I don't know. I can't figure it out.

—He's not like that, Mom.

She looks away from him, takes her scared eyes to the fire, to the shadows and light playing there.

—How would you know? she says. You didn't even know his wife had left him.

Nolan leaves the next morning while his mother waves goodbye from the front porch of the family home. Rounding the bend, he looks in the truck's side mirror and he sees she's still standing there, so he taps the horn twice and she raises her hand to him. Itinerant son, wayward again. A worried look about her mouth. Creases at the eyes. Finding a place for her hands. He's seen that look before and it's not stopped him.

Forty minutes later he's caught in traffic on the elevated

interstate cutting through Sacramento. The day is already warm. He told his mother he would visit Chance, four hours east in Sonoma County, but he'll take his time getting there and he won't stay long. At some point in their youth, after the fire, before their father's passing, the brothers grew apart. Chance became an articulate and social individual, confident in asserting his opinion regardless of whether he was wrong or right; he was just desperate to be heard. There was something he got from being heard. Nolan, though, Nolan turned inward. As distrustful of words as he was uncomfortable using them, he honed his skills of observation. At the family dinner table he sat quietly and listened to the debates Chance stirred with his parents. He took in their ideas and listened carefully to them, and then he watched his family away from the table to see what led to those ideas. His mother at the school library, reading at lunch when he'd swing in to visit, or working in her garden. Chance on the family phone, talking with friends late at night in his room, or sneaking out to smoke and to drink at Placerville Union, unaware that their father would be buried there in a decade's time. And, their father, corporate park custodian, sitting on the couch at night mock-yelling at the nightly news, working alongside their mother in the kitchen preparing dinner while the boys did homework at the kitchen table. As proud as their mother was of Chance following in her footsteps to Cal, so their father was of Nolan's wandering.

But would he still be proud? Even he settled down and married and started a family.

Crossing the Sacramento River in traffic, Nolan eavesdrops on the middle-aged man in the pickup next to him. The man also drives with his window down and his forearm resting on the door. He talks on his cell phone all the while.

—No, the man states. Absolutely not. Our response must continue to be, no.

In the next lane over, a tractor trailer bears an advertisement identical to that of a billboard looming above the overpass exchange ahead.

—I don't care about the collateral damage, the man says. OK? Over my dead body. That means never.

It's afternoon when Nolan enters the Coastal Range of northern California by way of an oak-lined back road. Black power lines weave through an irregular latticework of gnarled limbs while vineyards, rows recently mowed, line either side of the road. The squat brown vines glow at their spurs with the green hue of leafy shoots.

The last time he drove this road he'd come to the small town of Burnridge for his brother's wedding. Chance was working as a reporter at the local weekly newspaper and his fiancée had a small yoga studio across from the post office. They'd just bought, with his mother's assistance, an overpriced tract home. Nolan arrived in Burnridge just before the ceremony, and he left not long after the reception ended. Several months later he received a card at his PO box in Eureka that read:

Thanks for the toaster.

Despite his having gifted them a spiked carving platter he'd made from handsome slats of maple, walnut, and teak, and into which he'd burned their initials.

Just because you put effort into something, don't expect others to appreciate it, his mother said to him when he mentioned the card in one of their conversations. It might not be their thing.

Crossing the Sotoyome Valley floor the road straightens some and the cleft dome of Fumarole Peak, towering in the distance beneath a vague layer of cloud and haze, comes into full view. Nolan crosses a river bridge, and at the far end of the bridge a hand-painted sign reads:

BURNRIDGE CAMPGROUND—TRAILERS WELCOME

He finds the manager rolling sealant over one of two dozen or so picnic tables pushed together in a large clearing.

—We're closed until the First of May, the manager says without looking up from his work.

—I was wondering if maybe just for the night.

—That'll be fine in a week.

—I can pay cash.

—Like I said.

Nolan looks over the picnic tables.

—I tell you what, he says.

He finishes sealing the remaining tables by sunset. From inside the manager's double-wide comes the television broadcast of a baseball game underway in Los Angeles. An aluminum phone booth stands at the far end of the front porch, its fluorescent light flickering in the chrome-plated change box. Nolan stands looking at the phone booth. He knows Linda's probably getting ready for her shift. She's probably standing in front of the bathroom mirror wiping away steam, her hair up in a towel, the tightly coiled cord of her hair dryer hanging down, almost reaching the beige bathmat. On the counter, the small transistor radio tuned to public radio.

They never gave a name to what they shared, but, looking at the phone, he wants to believe she will know it was as significant for him as he believes it was for her. He also knows wanting something to be some way doesn't make it so.

Nolan raps on the four-by porch post at the entrance to the manager's double-wide. A yellow ribbon decal is peeling from the corner of a curtained window. A security camera, tucked in a corner of the porch awning, aimed at the door.

—Hold on a sec, the manager says from inside.

A moment later, he opens the screened door with a can of beer in each hand.

—Take a seat, he says, handing Nolan one of the cans before settling into a weathered armchair.

—Much obliged.

Nolan sits on the top step of the front porch, leans back against the railing, opens the beer, and takes a long slug. He finishes nearly half of it in one drink. He takes a second drink and then wipes his mouth on the back of his hand. It's quiet at the empty campground, verdant and clean, and the cool smells of dusk, so near to the river, are tinged by sealant.

—Tables look good, the manager says, stretching out a leg and massaging his knee.

—I used the last of your thinner cleaning up.

—They'll make more.

Down at the river, swallows weave through the bridge's rusty truss work.

—Nice and green out here, Nolan says after taking a sip of his beer.

—You'd never know we were in a drought.

The manager takes a sip of his beer and then rests the cold can on his knee.

—That rig of yours looks like it's covered some ground.

—Yes, sir.

—How long you had it?

—I've only had the Ranger a few years now, but I've had the trailer since I was nineteen.

—Ranger before they became minis.

—Yes, sir.

—Looks like you've done some work on the trailer.

—I have.

—I always like to see people take care of the old things. The things built right.

A quiet moment passes between the two men as an approaching vehicle's headlights throw truss shadows over the backs of Nolan's truck and trailer, parked below the sharp bend in the road at the entrance to the bridge. Shadows and light lean away from their origins and then back again as the car passes the entrance.

—How far is the ocean from here? Nolan asks.

—About an hour or so. That where you're headed?

—Eventually.

—Nice out there.

—That's how I remember it.

The manager looks into the mouth of his beer can.

—I usually have the gate open at dawn.

—Yes, sir.

—You know, if you're looking, there's plenty more work around here.

—I'm afraid I'm just passing through.

—Figured I'd offer.

—I appreciate it.

When Nolan finishes his beer, he stands and squashes the aluminum can beneath his boot.

—Leave it there, the manager says. I'll take care of it.

Nolan sets the squashed can on the porch railing, and the remaining beer trickles from a pinch in the can, out along the railing before soaking into the aged redwood.

—Thanks again for the hospitality.

—My pleasure. Enjoy the ocean.

—Thank you.

As Nolan is walking downhill, he hears the car approaching before he sees it. He's thinking about how if he were in any other town he'd stay and help the man. Swim in the river each morning and walk the surrounding vineyards each evening searching for arrowheads and coins. Maybe even settle in for the rest of the summer and watch the leaves change during the fall. But not here. Not mere miles from his brother.

He hears the vehicle accelerate. The first shadows of the bridge's truss work appear at the back of his trailer with the approaching headlights. It's almost dark down by the river, and the strength of the smell of the sealant has him thinking he'll continue on down past his truck and trailer to the river. Shadows grow tall along the back of the Airstream, but differently than before, Nolan notices, when tires screech and a convertible two-door coupe, nose-heavy and wheels spinning, launches off the road bank and slams down on the roof of his trailer. The impact drives the Ranger forward several feet into the trunk of a cottonwood, and propane immediately hisses from the tank at the front of the Airstream. A sizable widow-maker falls from the cottonwood canopy and shatters the Ranger's windshield.

—Holy shit, he hears the campground manager yell from the porch of his trailer. Did you see that?

Nolan runs to the wreck. The first thing he notices is

gasoline seeping from the convertible's undercarriage and slipping down shiny crimps in the trailer's crumpled side. That, and the engine, running at high RPMs, isn't shutting off.

As he reaches the convertible, the driver's-side door opens and a man steps out and falls to the mowed grass. A woman in the passenger seat collapses over the middle console, laughing, her face contorted and her hair disheveled.

—He fell, she says to Nolan but points at the man.

The engine noise seems to be getting louder, and although Nolan thinks about trying to find a way into his trailer to grab his photographs and his bankroll, he leaves the man on the ground and scrambles up on the roof of the trailer and into the convertible. He tries the ignition key but it won't budge. The woman looks at Nolan through glassy eyes, astonished that he's suddenly standing there. Her cheeks are flushed and blood runs from a laceration across the bridge of her nose.

—He fell, she states, her smile gone, her voice almost lost to the engine noise.

Nolan presses his handkerchief to the laceration and places her hand on it.

—Hold this, he says.

He tries to unclasp her seatbelt but it won't budge, so he takes his knife from his front-right pants' pocket, flicks it open with his thumb, and quickly saws the belt free with the serrated hilt of the blade, the woman's eyes wide at the sight of it. On the ground, the campground manager stands with his hand on the man's shoulder.

—We missed the turn, the woman says as Nolan lifts and pushes her from the wreckage of his home toward the manager.

Back on the ground, Nolan leaves the manager with the

couple and hurries toward the door to the Airstream, but the weight of the convertible has jarred it shut. He runs around to the front window, but in passing he notices flies gathering where propane spews. He can get through the window and reach at least his photos but the sound of the engine and the smell of the propane turns him back toward the manager and the couple.

—Let's get them back up from here, he says.

The campground manager grabs the woman by the arm and pulls her uphill while Nolan hauls the man to his feet and they stumble to the clearing where the picnic tables are arranged. The man sits on one of the benches.

—It's wet, he says, all child-like, but Nolan's already turning back toward his truck and trailer when the convertible's battery arcs, and a tremendous explosion of fire swells into the trees, obscuring the night's first stars.

Smaller fires settle in throughout the truck and Airstream and flames flicker in the grass at the base of the trailer where the gasoline has pooled. The tips of the low-lying limbs of the surrounding trees burn like tiny candles and uphill, where Nolan and the manager stand with the man and the woman, Nolan can feel the heat of the fire settle in among his possessions. He can feel it on his face and in the fabric and the pearl buttons of his flannel shirt.

—I'm going to call the fire department, the manager says, turning for his double-wide.

With the man and woman beside him, Nolan watches flames gust over shards of a stained-glass window he purchased in East Carbon, Utah. He installed the custom window to replace the broken, louvered original. Through the opening, he can see his dun-colored work hat, surrounded by flames.

Nolan takes a step toward the flames, but the woman places her hand on his forearm and stops him.

—No, she says. Don't.

4

Dawn, smelling of wood smoke and the sweet acridity of burnt synthetics. Nolan knocks a cabinet door free of its hinges with a spade shovel and a coffee can rolls down from the interior. The plastic lid has melted in on the can and fire has burned through most of Nolan's bankroll. He thumbs the flaking paper – twenties, fifties, hundreds – and then looks at the soot marks left on his hands. He throws the can, and when it doesn't break anything he picks up a brass bookend and throws it into a cabinet and smashes his dishware and drinking glasses. After the sound of breaking glass, the quiet of the river campground pervades.

Nolan prided himself on being a man free of possessions, but this was before he'd been freed of them. He stands there, looking over what's become of his belongings.

So smart you kept your savings in a coffee can. He shakes his head in disgust. Who did you think you were fooling?

He spends the better part of the morning prying and rooting with the shovel around what he can access of the trailer until he finds a flat, fireproof box. He brings the box out in the pan of the shovel and sets it on the ground and kneels beside it and checks uphill toward the manager's trailer before he lifts the lid to reveal a snub-nosed .38 revolver and six shiny brass cartridges. The revolver has survived the fire intact, the bullets still usable. Nolan wraps some sooty clothing around the box and places it in a black plastic trash sack.

Robins, picking at the grass, scatter suddenly as a '69 Valiant pulls into the campground and slowly makes its way down to the clearing.

—Shit, Nolan mutters, recognizing the vehicle immediately.

Resting against the handle of the shovel, he nudges up the brim of his Western hat and the soot on his fingertips smudges the clean white brim. The car parks and Chance, dressed in brown corduroys, a rumpled white dress shirt, and a thin red-and-blue striped tie, loosely knotted at the neck, climbs out. He is tall and slender and in need of a shave. His hair is disheveled and he wears thick black-rimmed prescription glasses. From atop the Valiant's dash he retrieves a digital camera and a spiral notepad. He closes the door to the vehicle with a screech and a thud and while he saunters downhill, he rolls back the cuffs on his shirt with a pen in his hand. He rolls the cuffs of his shirt out, not in, as Nolan does, as their father did.

—This where the accident took place? he says with a wry smile.

—If you want to call it that.

—What would you call it?

—Carelessness.

This was something their father used to say to them as children. Chance adjusts his glasses, and smiles more freely.

—I came out as soon as I saw your name in the police blotter this morning. You all right?

—This what passes for news around these parts?

—Yeah, I'd say it stands a pretty good chance of making it above this week's fold. What are you doing here?

—Mom asked me to swing through.

—And you agreed?

—She said you and Dawn split up.

Chance runs his tongue over a molar.

—What I want to know is why didn't you punch the guy out?

—It wasn't worth it.

—Some drunk and his mistress destroy all your shit and you just stand there?

—I didn't know she was his mistress.

—Neither did his wife. But that's beside the point. You should have clocked him.

—I guess I'm not as emotional as you are, Chance.

—I go by Cosmo, Nolan. Don't provoke.

—Must've slipped my mind.

—Nothing slips your mind. You're just being a butthead.

—Look who's provoking.

—I'm on deadline.

Chance steps forward and pushes a button on the top of his camera and the lens extends from the tiny plastic box.

—I thought you were a scribbler, Nolan says.

—Picture's worth a thousand words.

—Depends on who's stringing them together, I reckon.

Dust motes swirl through canted bars of sunlight surrounding the men. Cosmo tilts his head, squints through his glasses, and smiles at Nolan with a condescending air he knows will irritate his brother. In the distance, a robin sings.

—You *reckon*? Cosmo says.

—That's right.

—Well, I *reckon* that unless this is your property we're standing on, I can take all the pictures I want.

—You know I'd rather you didn't.

—Why? You running from the law, cowboy?

—I look like a bad guy to you, egghead?

Cosmo steps forward and rights a reading lamp, positions it near a mirror, and then squats to shoot them from a low angle, having positioned the lamp and the mirror as if they were the only things that didn't get blown over or destroyed by the explosion and the fire. Nolan steps forward and shoves the tip of the shovel pan in the ground directly before Cosmo and sets his boot on the tang so it obscures the reporter's shot.

—Don't misrepresent this.

—What, the lamp?

—Yes, the lamp and the mirror.

—It looks better this way.

—But that ain't how it was.

Cosmo presses the button on the top of the camera and the lens retracts, the tiny sounds of gears grating in that small plastic skull. He stands and crosses his arms and then brings his hand to his mouth for a second before gesturing away from it as he speaks:

—How is it that we both attended the same grammar, middle, and high school, both grew up in the same house, with the same parents, and yet you end up using *reckon* and *ain't*? Talk about misrepresentation.

Nolan doesn't respond. Cosmo adjusts his eyeglasses and the two brothers stare one another down for a second or two before Cosmo says:

—You need a ride into town.

—I'm all right, but thanks for the offer.

—I wasn't offering. It was a simple declarative sentence.
—I'd rather walk.
—You do that.
—I will.
—All right then.
—OK.

An air of cultivated leisure pervades the Burnridge Plaza. Laughter peals from the patio seating areas of several restaurants around the square. Between the restaurants, storefronts with glittering window displays offer high-end furniture, cooking utensils, jewelry, geodes, indigenous artifacts, bamboo-fiber men's shirts, women's silk scarves and exotic leather shoes, antiques, and objects fashioned to resemble antiques. Very few of the items for sale on the plaza have been mass-produced, and even those that have are of high quality and few in number.

Nolan looks around the Spanish-style plaza. Two broad walkways run diagonally from each corner of the square. Where the walkways intersect, a fountain burbles at the center of a shallow rectangular pool. The plaza grass is freshly cut and water lingers in the cuts of the recently hosed-off concrete walkways. Harp music emanates daintily from the chandelier-lit, open-air lobby of a hotel across the plaza from where Nolan stands, and the aromatics of brick-oven wood smoke, caramelizing onions, baking bread, and roasting coffee beans infuse the evening with a richness he's experienced when passing through other premier tourist destinations.

Nolan scans the storefronts for the office of the *Burnridge Observer*. When he finds it, he reaches down for his sack and notices, at the foot of the bench, several unfiltered cigarettes that have been smoked down to nubs. Nolan shoulders the sack and moves on.

The newspaper office is flanked by a bookstore and a lingerie boutique. A black-and-white notice posted in the front window reads: *$1,000 for information leading to the arrest and conviction of the individual(s) responsible for arsons set in Burnridge since Feb. 29.* Alongside this notice, a glossy bulletin advertises for locals to be cast as extras in a major motion picture that will begin filming in a little more than two months' time.

Nolan removes his hat as he steps inside the office and greets a female secretary. Two rows of desks line the walls behind her, separated by a walkway that leads to a door at the back of the room.

—Evening, Nolan says. I'm looking for Chance Jackson.

—There's no one here by that name.

—Cosmo, Nolan says a bit impatiently. I'm looking for Cosmo Swift.

—He's in his office.

Nolan looks over the room of empty desks.

—Which one's that?

Pointing out the front door, the secretary says:

—Three doors down.

In the dim light of The Bull and The Bear, Cosmo sits with a confusion of pages spread out over the dead center of the empty bar. He has a red pencil in one hand and a bottle of beer in the other. A copper Zippo lighter that belonged to their father stands upright on the bar, a paper weight to his notes.

Nolan takes a seat two down from Cosmo, and Cosmo speaks to him without looking up from the pages:

—Thirsty?

—That a question or a simple declarative sentence?

—No, that was a question.

—Then, yes, I am.

—Dave, Cosmo yells to the bartender, who was on a stool at the end of the bar doing the crossword but is now standing before the two brothers.

—What can I get you? the bartender asks Nolan.

—Whiskey and a half draft back.

—This one's on me, Dave.

—Stop the press.

—Friend-o here's had a stroke of bad luck.

—Since when do you have any friends, Cosmo?

The bartender turns to the plastic draft handles, shiny and bright and perpendicular to the bar, and Cosmo leans over the stool between him and Nolan, nods toward Dave, and whispers hoarsely:

—Absolutely hates it when you order anything he can't twist the cap off of. Some nights, I come in here and order nothing but Mojitos.

—Good to know you're still in the habit of making things easy on folks.

Cosmo sits back and looks Nolan in the eye and they stay locked like that until Cosmo hikes his glasses up the bridge of his nose. He picks up the Zippo, snaps it open, and deftly strikes the flint. Holding the flame between them, he says:

—Everyone thought our firebug got you.

Nolan nods toward Cosmo's beer.

—How many of those you had already?

—We don't keep count around here.

Cosmo snaps the lighter shut and palms it flat on the bar just as the bartender sets the beer and a shot glass on a napkin before Nolan. Pulling an unlabeled fifth from the well before him, the bartender pours the shot as Cosmo speaks:

—See, what the denizens of our fair and wealthy hamlet fail to recognize in this era of lucrative expansion is that this arsonist of ours is a long time in coming. We've lost track of all that is right and good because we've been so busying fleecing the tourists. We've lost sight of who we were and we've accepted that it's convenient to ignore who we are. We deserve this hero's indignation. We've earned it. You buy that, Dave?

—I stopped listening to you beers ago, Cosmo.

—You still read my articles, though, right?

—Only when I'm cleaning the bird cage.

Cosmo waves the bartender off as the man returns to his stool and lifts his pencil and crossword. Nolan raises the shot glass, shoots it, and chases it down with a good long slug of the cold beer.

—So, Cosmo says.

—So, Nolan responds.

—You've done your mother's bidding. Here I am. What now?

—What now?

—What's your fall back plan?

—It went up in flames.

—Well, you're welcome to stay with me until you get back on your feet.

—Thanks, but I'm just passing through.

Cosmo nods.

—My offer stands.

—Thank you.

A quiet moment passes between the brothers until a song plays on the jukebox to remind patrons it's standing in a far corner, illuminated. Nolan scans the bar.

—They serve any food here?

—Hot nuts and cocks of salami.

—Very funny.

—I wasn't trying to be funny. Those are your food options.

Nolan nods in the direction of the papers spread out before Cosmo.

—What's new?

—This? Same old, same old. Retirees don't want to pay taxes for schools their kids are too old to attend, and locals are angry there's no place to park downtown. Did you know scientists discovered a new species of hummingbird in Colombia?

—Can't say that I did.

—And, they may have identified the genetic sequence for bipolar disorder.

—OK.

Cosmo squints through his eyeglasses as he speaks:

—What's any of this have to do with the price of crude in China?

—I don't follow.

—Yes, you do, but that's beside the point. The bajillion-dollar question is, or, rather, questions are: what happened to my marriage, and is Cosmo née Chance all right in the head?

—You expect her to be OK, way you rattle on?

—Mom frets.

—Maybe because you've given her ample reason to.

—And you haven't?

—I at least make some attempt to conceal my eccentricities.

Cosmo spews beer spittle over the pages before him. Wiping off his mouth, he says:

—Who knew you even knew the word, let alone how to use it in a sentence?

—What happened to your marriage, Chance?

—Dawn left me for our real-estate agent.

—Why?

—He's got a tremendous schlong. I don't fucking know.

—You don't know?

—We fell out of love, Nolan. Shit, man.

—We?

—She. OK. She fell out of love with me and in love with our real-estate agent and his tanned, tattooed torso and his blinding veneer.

—Veneer?

—This thing they do to teeth nowdays. Makes them all shiny and white. Thirteen hundred bucks a tooth.

—Why do you know that?

—I live alone, Nolan. Late at night I sit before the Internet and ask it questions.

Cosmo shrugs.

—It's a cultural fucking phenomenon, you ignoramus. You see it on TV people all the time. It's especially obvious when you watch reality TV, just how unnatural the veneer looks.

—I don't watch much TV.

—You should. It tells us who we are.

—Maybe you.

—Because you're removed from all this? Above it all? I forget sometimes.

—I'm sorry to hear Dawn left you, Cosmo. I am.

—Guy sells me an overpriced house and then steals my wife. Awesome. If it happened to anyone else, I'd be laughing.

—No, you wouldn't.

—Yes, I would. Sometimes I even say it aloud, like it belongs to someone else, and it does make me laugh.

—Well.

—Get this, she said they "formed an intense spiritual connection." From where language like this even entered her vocabulary, I am at a complete loss.

—People change.

—And how. Last I heard, they moved to Costa Rica and she opened a yoga studio. Fake Teeth teaches surfing, now. The same woman used to hassle me about developing and maintaining a solid retirement plan.

Nolan responds by nodding slightly and staring at the bar. Cosmo turns away from him and Nolan looks up at his brother's profile in the bar lights, and the different colors of all the bottles lined up across from them, and he sees the lights and bottles mirrored in the lenses of Cosmo's eyeglasses, the images wavering along the stems of the plastic frames.

—You at all familiar with the philosophical notion of nihilism? Cosmo asks.

—I might've encountered it under a different handle.

—You see, Cosmo says as he raises one hand, palm up, like the scalepan of a balance. With the loss of meaning we create, he says, raising the other hand even with the first. Or we destroy.

He drops both hands on the mess of papers on the bar, the tip of the red pencil aimed away from him, their father's Zippo on its side.

—I mean, I understand and accept that the world is not black and white. I understand that sincerity can be dangerous and that irony can be a tool of empire, that people who profess to be open-minded rarely are, and that if a monarch smashes flat on a windshield in Monterey, all of California south of the Transverse Range will break off into the Pacific Ocean. I will accept all that. But, superstitious hippies and willfully ignorant rednecks are fucking this country up, Nolan.

—Chance—

—And mark my words, brother, this red/blue shit doesn't change, and pronto, you can bet your ass we're headed for dark times. Dark times, indeed.

Cosmo picks up the lighter and taps the bottom edge of it once, twice on the bar.

—But not on my watch. No way.

With his elbows rested on the bar, Cosmo lifts his beer to his mouth and shrugs.

—I did, however, get a sweet bachelor pad out of the deal. Surrender your earthly possessions and whatnot.

He drinks. Then:

—As long as I can keep up with the mortgage.

Nolan leans over the seat between them and places his hand on his brother's shoulder.

—Let's get you home, Chance.

—Nolan, I may be drunk, but I will sock you in the mouth hard and repeatedly if you don't stop calling me Chance. I go by Cosmo, partner, respect that.

Over Cosmo's shoulder, Nolan can see the bartender eyeing them suspiciously over the fold of his crossword, so Nolan leans back and nods at the man.

—What're you doing here, Nolan? Cosmo asks, his voice raised. What do you really, actually, literally want from me?

—I'm here to ask you nicely to keep my name out of the paper.

—Why?

—Just how I am.

—Mr Low Profile.

—Something like that.

Cosmo smiles and shakes his head.

—Do you really think I'd do that to you? Like I don't know my own brother?

Nolan clenches his jaw and stares into the glass in front of him. Cosmo says:

—Buy me a beer and let's talk about something else already.

—All right.

—Dave, Cosmo calls out to the bartender.

—What now?

—Another round, *por favor.*

—Here I am hoping you were going to settle up and leave.

—No chance.

Nolan awakes the next morning hung over and sprawled out on a love seat in Cosmo's garage. His boots and hat are still on and the bath mat he used for a blanket smells of mildew and toothpaste. The hen-peck rhythm of animated typing punctuates the morning calm. When Nolan finally focuses his eyes, he sees that he is surrounded by a jumble of thrift-store house furniture and uneven stacks of plain cardboard moving boxes.

Suddenly, he remembers the snub-nosed revolver, and he scrambles for the black plastic sack until he finds the fireproof box hidden among his soot-covered clothes. He sinks back in the love seat and tries to relax, but his head aches some and his throat is dry and his tongue swollen.

Nolan just sits for a bit, idly working saliva from his cheeks while looking down at the calluses on his hands. He has no bank account and no home to speak of. He carelessly abandoned the potential for love with a good woman, and other than those tiny, hard lumps along the tops of his palms and the segments of his fingers, all that he has to show for thirteen years as a journeyman carpenter has been destroyed by fire. The money he will be compensated for the loss of his tools and his belongings, for his truck and the Airstream trailer, is going to be insufficient; it's going to be insulting. Over the years he fashioned a philosophy from observation and experience and contemplation and lashed it to the fundamental notion that beginning and end are words as apt to explain the machinations of the world as are good and evil. Change is the only constant and the world is a perpetual state of flux. Plain-spoken words unravel truths the same as riddles, only different.

But at times like this, ideas like these are awfully difficult to accept.

Nolan stands and stashes the box containing the .38 and the cartridges beneath one of the love seat's cushions. When he opens the door to the house, the sound of the typing becomes considerably louder. The bedroom door at the far end of the hallway is open, and Nolan can see clothes lying on the floor. The doors to the second and third bedrooms are closed, and from behind one of these comes the typing noise. Other than light sneaking around the curtain in Cosmo's bedroom window, the hallway is dim. Nolan stands listening to the typing for a moment because there's a persistence and eagerness to it that complements Cosmo's verve. The sound is a signature of sorts.

Nolan turns and walks the few steps to the living room. He finds the room empty except for a leather recliner and a large flat-screen television set placed directly on the faux-wood flooring. On the screen, the first-person view from inside the cockpit of a spaceship paused in the midst of an interstellar battle. Laser beams hatch the starry background. Music issues faintly from the television's speakers, the few notes barely audible beneath the typing and caught in a loop that runs contrary to the excitement of the halted action. To the left of the recliner, an ashtray overflows with smoked joints.

Nolan crosses the room to the kitchen, where the countertops are bare save for a stained coffee maker and a toaster noisy with crumbs. The only cabinet that isn't empty is the one above the dishwasher; the door to the cabinet has been removed and the few plates and bowls that are in it are stacked awkwardly. The rest of Cosmo's dishes appear to be in the sink and each one resembles a painter's palette: pasta sauce, microwaved burrito remnants, frozen pizza pocket innards, chicken fried rice. Nolan looks at the dishes in the sink and then back into the living room. The only chair in the house appears to be the recliner. Nolan shakes his head.

After pouring himself a cup of lukewarm coffee, he stands for some time just looking out the sliding glass door at a small backyard, where a raised garden bed, overgrown with weeds and gone to seed, runs along the back fence. He remembers his mother mentioning that Dawn kept a garden. More than that, though, he remembers the desperate tone of his mother's voice when she told Nolan before his brother's wedding that she thought Dawn was good for Cosmo. Nolan remembers how desperate she was to believe the meaning behind her own words.

When the typing stops, the office door creaks open and seconds later Cosmo walks into the kitchen wearing a threadbare robe and fuzzy slippers. Nolan keeps his eyes fixed on a shovel leaning against the fence, the handle splintering in the weather and sun. It's irresponsible, treating tools that way,

Dawn's garden or not. Their father taught them better.

—Morning, partner, Cosmo drawls, smelling of marijuana smoke. How's the dome?

—It's been awhile since I closed a bar.

—Yeah, well, we could've gone home early with those two transplant cougars if you hadn't vomited in the hideous one's clutch.

—I never did that.

—You certainly looked like you might.

Cosmo pours the last of the coffee into a 32-oz convenience-store mug. Then he opens the freezer door and takes two frozen waffles from a torn cardboard box. The box is sticky with frozen orange juice concentrate that leaks from a container that was squashed by a liter of vodka.

—Breakfast? Cosmo offers Nolan a frozen waffle, encrusted with ice.

—You actually eat that crap?

—Not when I can afford to be choosy, no.

—It's cheaper to make them from scratch.

—Well, sweetheart, now that you've got all the time in the world on your hands, I'll expect soft-boiled *huevos* in bed.

Cosmo places the waffles in the toaster slots, depresses the lever, and leaves Nolan alone in the kitchen to listen to the toaster coils redden. His head is splitting now and his stomach is queasy and the coffee only seems to be making him feel worse. He places both hands on the kitchen counter, lowers his head, and closes his eyes. Soon, the toilet flushes on the other side of the wall and water runs through the copper pipes and Cosmo begins to sing in the shower. Nolan opens the refrigerator door in hopes of ice water but the light is blinding and the refrigerator is nearly empty. The only items are a torn cardboard twelve-pack of domestic light beer and a few condiments in glass jars and plastic squeeze bottles. An assortment of single-serving packets of parmesan cheese, chili-pepper flakes, soy sauce, and chili oil fill the butter tray.

Nolan closes the door and leans against the refrigerator. There isn't a decoration on it, not a photo or a coupon or even a magnet. Spider webs glom to a corner of the window above the sink, and dead flies lie on their backs in a bed of finger-smoothed caulk that runs the length of a paint-brushed windowsill. The entire house appears to have been packed up and stored in the boxes in the garage. Only what Cosmo has deemed the barest of necessities remain. Nolan tries to remember the last time, if ever, he was in a tract home that he didn't help construct; in one that was actually lived in; in one that had already housed a marriage and a divorce.

When Cosmo re-enters the kitchen, he is wearing the same shirt and tie and corduroys from the day before. The waffles have popped, and he tucks one into his shirt pocket and stuffs the other in his mouth. Under his arm he has a clutter of papers, his digital camera, and his notepad.

—I'm going to head out to the campground later today, Nolan says. I want to be there when they haul my stuff off.

—You want a ride out?

—No, I figured I'd walk.

—There's a bike in the garage. You're welcome to it.

—I never took to motorcycles.

—Yeah, it's not that kind of bike.

Stashed against a wall of the garage, behind some cardboard boxes full of empty picture frames and unlit candles and pack-aged linens, Nolan uncovers a woman's ten-speed bicycle, shiny and pink. He inflates the tires, oils the chain, tightens the brakes, and checks the nuts at the front and back forks. After hiding the .38 at the bottom of a box labeled KITCH, Nolan puts on his hat, rolls back the garage door, and raises his hand against the glaring sun.

The streets of Valley Oaks Estates are lined with mottled-bark sycamore, leafing out. Every fourth or fifth house has an identical floor plan, but painted a different color. Just by looking at the fronts of the tract houses, Nolan can tell that most of them are three bedrooms, two baths. They all have two-car garages facing the street and floor plans Nolan can rough frame in his sleep. Vehicles, aimed in different directions, dot the landscape and the drone of traffic from Highway 101, which runs north–south at the western edge of the once-rural farm town, is light enough to be almost unnoticeable. Cars are parked in the driveways or along the streets because so many of the garages are full of relatively inexpensive, plastic, imported stuff.

—Stuffed with stuff, his father said once when Nolan asked why their family's garage was so empty compared to others he'd seen in the tracts surrounding Sacramento. People like having stuff, his father said, having fun with the word.

—Stuff, the child Nolan said.

—Stuff.

As Nolan reaches the intersection at the end of Cosmo's long block, he notices a service banner hanging in the front window of a corner home. White field with red border. Two blue stars. One for each child. Flag his father's mother never flew. Nolan leans into the turn and glides effortlessly through the four-way stop, hung over and stranded, reading himself into the story of the banner. These are the people you've been building for, he thinks, righting the bicycle. Evidence of the wars all around him; evidence of ignorance of them, as well.

It's a nice, safe place, Valley Oaks, and Nolan knows Cosmo and his ex-wife lived beyond their means to buy in.

CONSERVE WATER, a sign reads at the center of a dead lawn, only the dandelion weeds green. He rides past yards recently mulched with stained wood chips and planted with drought-resistant shrubs, by rocks gardened by Occidentals. Only in their landscaping are the tract houses unique, but similar in that the majority of the plants are purely ornamental.

—People expect the shelves to stay stocked, an old timer explained it to him once when he asked why tract developers never plant fruit trees. That, the man said, and it's not cost effective.

—Doesn't seem very smart, Nolan responded.

—Let's see how you feel about that when you're the one signing the checks.

—Nah, that's not for me.

—Then keep your head down and hammer away, nobody.

Nolan rides with the wind in his face and the fresh air alleviates his hangover some. He pedals to the edge of the sub-division, where a low hill overlooks the town of Burnridge, settled by easterners as a way station for travelers heading east to the Sierras or south to San Francisco from Oregon. A town of 8,000 nestled in the confluence of three of the world's premier wine-grape growing valleys. Coastal Range hills of oak and fir, of second-growth redwood. Nolan stops there for a moment to gain his bearings.

Across the street and down the hill lie the older parts of the town. The street before him is a marker in the geology of the place, a stratum of materials and designs. Behind him, to the north, is Valley Oaks, and to the south, over the simple rooflines of mostly postwar homes, stand the ornate flourishes of the heritage homes: the intricate roof-cuts of the Queen Annes and Victorians; original California bungalows and refurbished Italianate mansions, all at the outskirts of the plaza. Citrus and apple trees grow in the front yards there, persimmon and plum. Some of the paint jobs have six or seven colors. Nolan can see copper gutters and steep slate roofs. One or two of the old houses are being restored, and the new wood shines under the sun.

He pushes the bicycle forward and rides west and then north on Burnridge Avenue. He rides away from the plaza, away from the older, more affluent part of town. At the north end he pedals past an automotive dealership, a gas station and quick mart, a muffler shop, and a Chinese restaurant. He continues beyond the city limits to the countryside, where vineyards in every direction run up from the valley floor to the serrated ridges. Poppies and lupine and wild oats line the shoulders of the road. The stalks of the oats already showing blond at their bases. In the distance, Fumarole Peak stands alone above the foothills, its crown darkened by chaparral, by trees and shrubs that, when stressed for water, infuse the atmosphere around them with an inflammable essence.

Nolan coasts down the mile-long straightaway. He's not looking forward to seeing the convertible on the back of the Airstream like some piggybacking parasite, his truck torched. Just before the railroad crossing, before the road turns east toward the river through vineyard and pasture-land, a pot-holed gravel road leads up to the crown of a low knoll where a rundown two-story farmhouse, white with green trim, stands among a cluster of blue oaks. A Ram is parked in front of the neglected farmhouse, the only structure for miles around.

Nolan slows to the side of the asphalt when he sees the truck and stops in the shade of several tall eucalyptus at the entrance to the gravel road. Cicada sound from the trees. Crickets in the frail grass. Sunlight sneaks through the oak canopy and glints off the Ram's lumber rack. A crow alights on the power line that runs up to the farmhouse and *caaws* down at the journeyman.

Nolan sits uncomfortably on the bicycle seat, just looking up at the work truck and at the old house. He has one boot on the gravel shoulder and the other on a bicycle pedal. The shadow of his hat and profile are cast out to the side of him and he looks up at the sun and then back down at his shadow.

He's been in situations like this before, but none as hapless. The towing crew won't be at the campground for at least another hour. He has little money and no transportation. His prospects are slim. And there's something about Cosmo he's unsure of, something he feels he needs to stick around a short while to figure out. He exhales through his nostrils and then turns the bicycle onto the gravel road.

Opposite the back porch of the farmhouse, strands of lichen sway in the breeze like powder-green scarves of lace. Nolan leans the bicycle against the trunk of one of the oaks, removes his hat, and dabs the sweat from his brow with his handkerchief. PACIFIC WIND CARPENTRY is written on the driver's-side door of the pickup. As Nolan approaches the house, a figure stirs within. The front door is missing, and from the shadows emerges a deeply suntanned man with shoulder-length, sandy-blond hair and light blue eyes. He wears a serape with a beer logo over his heart and he reeks of marijuana smoke.

—Morning, Nolan says, touching the brim of his hat. You starting a project here?

—You with the county? the man asks.

Nolan looks down the gravel road, then over at the woman's bicycle resting pink against the tree.

—Yeah, he says, I'm here to check your permits.

That night, Nolan sits in the passenger seat of Cosmo's Valiant as they drive down Burnridge Avenue toward the plaza. In a far corner of the sky, trapped beneath a low-lying, dense layer of fog, the yellow-orange glow of a house fire looms above the black composite rooftops and silhouetted power lines.

—How many of these has he set?

—Five, Cosmo says, raising a hand, the other one resting on the steering wheel and holding a long, skinny joint.

Nolan whistles a short note.

—But there's only so many left to burn.

—How's that?

—He's only burning the old ones, the last of the heritage homes the transplants up from the city buy and remodel as weekend homes or retirement projects.

—That's too bad.

—And that's debatable.

—You really think it's OK to go around burning down history?

—I think it's political. An act of defiance. He'd rather see the Victorians and bungalows burn to the ground than the tourists move in, even part time, and take over the town's history.

—And you know this how?

—Because I've been paying close attention.

Cosmo offers the joint to Nolan.

—I'm all right.

—Suit yourself.

Cosmo throws the joint out the window.

—That easy to come by out here? Nolan asks.

—Shit grows on trees.

Nolan looks out the window and up at the sky, socked in by the marine layer that follows the river upstream and comes in from the coast most summer nights. The marine layer glows from all the lights of the town, and the spot above where the fire burns glows even brighter.

—Fog is something else here, Nolan says, but Cosmo doesn't respond, he's so fixated on the spot above the fire.

Nolan studies his brother's reflection in the windshield. He can see the corners of Cosmo's eyes squinting, his look pensive, determined. Finally, Cosmo says:

—You actually go out on that bicycle today, wearing that hat and all?

—What's wrong with my hat?

—Sun's done gone down, partner.

Cosmo smiles, driving with one hand resting on the Valiant's steering wheel and the other out the window, feeling the air on an upturned palm.

—You call Mom yet? Cosmo asks.

—No.

—You want me to?

—I figured we'd both call her this weekend.

—Which implies you'll still be here by then.

Nolan looks down at his hands and then ahead through the Valiant's dirty windshield. Windows, flickering blue from the televisions turned on inside, stand out along the streetscape.

—I happened on this remodel today, Nolan says. On the way out to the campground. Contractor there agreed to take me on as low man.

—What's a low man?

—Means I do the grunt work.

—Grunt work, Cosmo says. I like that.

—Yeah, well, it's not like I can be all that choosy.

—Not wasting any time, are you?

—Never saw much point in it.

Cosmo stops the Valiant at a four-way stop. The Valiant is the only car at the intersection, the only car on the street that isn't parked, but Cosmo doesn't drive forward. A porch light shines on an ornamental plum at the end of its bloom. A mosaic of tiny pink petals fractured by black limbs and purple leaves. Cosmo stares at the tree.

—Thing is, Nolan says, I was wondering if maybe you'd be willing to put me up for a spell. I'll pay you some as I get it, keep my space clean, and do chores around the place. Maybe even restore that garden out back. Just until I can get some money saved up to move on.

Cosmo continues to stare at the plum tree, radiant in the incandescent porch light.

—The garden was her thing, he says and then drives the Valiant through the intersection.

Nolan takes off his hat and places it on his knee.

—Stay as long as you want, Cosmo says, his mood picking up suddenly. Stay until the bank forecloses on us. We'll go down together, the Brothers Jackson.

Nolan hears the sound of a distant siren heading in the direction of the fire.

—You sure? Nolan asks.

Cosmo leans forward to peer at the fire's glow through an intricate network of power lines.

—*Mi casa es su casa.*

—Thank you.

—No problemo. I'd offer to throw out the boxes, but the mediator got me to agree not to for at least the first year of the divorce.

—Why?

—In case this isn't final.

—You mean like you two might get back together?

—Yes.

—You see that happening?

—No.

—You want that to happen?

Cosmo sighs.

—No. And, I don't want to talk about it anymore. I talk about it enough in my own head.

When Cosmo sits back, Nolan says:

—So what's this I hear about Russian sailors?

—Mom told you about that?

—That, and I heard you hammering away this morning.

—You really want to know?

—Only if you want to tell it.

Cosmo settles into his seat as the street-lamp lights pass over his mostly shadowed face.

—Well, for about a decade now I've been extrapolating the geopolitical ramifications of an obscure naval battle that took place between Russia and Japan in 1905.

—A decade is a long time.

—Yeah, well, there's been a lot of research to do.

—I don't know nothing about it.

—You sure this isn't boring you?

—Shit, I can't recall the last time I was bored.

—Lucky you.

—Go on.

—English-speaking historians refer to it as the Battle of Tsushima. It was the first encounter between armor-clad, steam-driven battleships.

—So you're writing a book?

Cosmo hunches toward the steering wheel again.

—No, he says, this is more than a book. Books are relics, fetish items, and this is a movie that can't be made because a screen can never encompass it.

—So what's the story?

—The story's not important.

—Since when?

—This isn't for everyone, Nolan.

—Who's it for, then?

—It's not for anyone in particular. It's just not for everyone.

With his wrists resting on the steering wheel and his hands out over the dashboard, Cosmo begins to gesture as he speaks:

—See, by my calculus, the repercussions of Tsushima have factored in events as significant and diverse as Hiroshima and Nagasaki, peak oil, Levittown, and the caves at Tora Bora. But also in the development of things as seemingly insignificant and unrelated as the action figure and Big Data. But even before that, there are all these interconnected stimuli coursing through hyperlinked synapses that strengthen with each fire to construct this macrocosmic loom, a real nightmare web of knowing, the loom itself a delicate weave, weaving through weaves already woven.

—But what happens?

Cosmo takes his hands from the steering wheel and runs them though his hair.

—Don't be such a literalist. I'm talking about the rendering of an event the world itself has already rendered. It's about tragedy and hubris. The transmigration of our souls to virtual reality. It's about overzealous technophiles and solutionists and attempts to realign the trajectories of meteors using nuclear warheads. And you want to know the story? The story is dark matter, autism, binary, the Great Game. It's about the influence of the English language on globalization. About lions and tigers and bears. All of it. We're talking about an event where the mostly nameless participants are long since dead, devoured by the gaping maw of History.

—I can see why it would take you so long.

—It's overwhelming, you know? It's like this elemental tide of weighted signals proliferating into a three-dimensional mosaic of color, color cast in a spectrum only my eyes seem capable of discerning, because of what? The kaleidoscope that is the language I speak? An experience I had as a child watching three men burn to death? A high-ceilinged library at Cal where I read *Mad* magazine when I was supposed to be reading works by the dead white men whose names were carved in stone and placed in the upper reaches of that solemn room?

Nolan watches his brother's hands. It's as if they're lifting the ends of threads from the air above the dashboard, as if threads are there to be lifted.

—The moment in time is like this kernel of data on the verge of being lost over the event horizon and into the Singularity. It's right there before me, just folding and unfold-ing like an expanding and contracting universe that mirrors our own understanding of said universe, a complex motion resembling something as simple as the involuntary act of breathing, but a breathing that's as deafening as the sound of our sun in space. No beginning, no end. As above, as below. *Omnia ab uno. Omnia ad unum* . . . But an arsonist—

Cosmo shakes his index finger toward the fire glow, his glasses crooked at this point.

—Now, there's a dude who gets it. Most of the fools around here, all hoping to bump their heads on something authentic, they don't recognize that all of this is just a sham. There's a reason they want to make movies here, man: the façade's already in place. But the arsonist understands this. He knows.

—Knows what?

—Let the Phoenix rise, man. Be the wind beneath its wings.

When they arrive at the scene of the house fire, red and blue lights carousel across the curtained windows and front-door plates. A crowd has gathered behind the yellow cordon tape while firemen work their way to and from the periphery of the fire.

Cosmo climbs out of the Valiant, walks directly toward the yellow line, and ducks under it without hesitation. Nolan eases out of the vehicle and closes the heavy door behind him. He walks along the sidewalk toward the cordon, weaving through shoulders coming and going, fingers pointing and mouths moving, everything generated by this particular spectacle.

—You know what this is? Nolan overhears a man say to the woman standing beside him.

—An old house burning to the ground, the woman says.

—No, this is terrorism.

—It's probably some kid desperate for attention.

—If so, he's got mine.

Water, running along the gutter, reflects the light of the flames that reach out of a second-story dormer and into myrtle limbs, wet from the firemen's efforts. Upstairs, double-hung windows are coated with soot and, downstairs, the lathed front-porch posts are charred timber. A hole has been chainsawed in the roof, and Nolan watches flames cling to the rafters, to the porcelain insulators. Tiny orange sparks flutter through the dark interior of the house. It saddens Nolan to see such an old home destroyed. Old ideas and efforts and memories going with it.

More than the fire, though, Nolan watches his brother. Cosmo is crouched beside the back end of one of the engines with the digital camera held up to his face. The flash from the photographs he takes momentarily lights the reflectors on the jacket sleeves of a group of firemen standing in the foreground. He lowers the camera to adjust the dials and the buttons. When Cosmo raises it again, Nolan sees the bright light of what must be flames, stilled, but pictured waving violently in the tiny display screen. The screen shines brightly in the reporter's face, the world's light having squeezed through a pinhole to fill it, flat as a page and completely illuminated.

5

To his first day of work on the farmhouse, Nolan brings nothing more than his lunch packed in a white plastic grocery sack that he's tied to the bicycle's handlebars. He finds Joe, the contractor who hired him, sitting in the cab of his Ram reading a surfing magazine and sipping yerba mate from a hollowed gourd.

—Not even a hammer, bro? Joe says on Nolan's approach.

—No, sir.

Joe tosses the magazine on the dash.

—You don't have to call me, sir, man. We don't have those hierarchies here. It messes with the energy of the place.

Straightaway, Joe has Nolan under the farmhouse, digging new footings with Manny, the other low man, both of them working side by side on their hands and knees beneath cob-webbed girders and old true-dimension redwood joists. It's hot, dusty, mindless work among fat black widows and sharp concrete clods, splintered dog bones, and the frayed insulation of sagging 110 lines.

To shed some light on the digging, Manny hangs a 150-watt droplight from a nail stuck in a joist, and the light sways from side to side between them each time Guillermo,

Manny's older brother and Joe's foreman, lets the cut ends of arsenic-soaked four-by-fours fall on the floorboards overhead. Guillermo is a small bull of a man with a receding hairline and a buzz cut, a man Nolan will only ever see smile once. Each time Guillermo drops one of the cut ends of the four-bys directly above their heads, Manny curses at him in Spanish and pounds the undersides of the flooring with his fist, causing even more dust to fall and to surround the low men in a dazzle of roiling motes, backlit by the droplight.

When Nolan first sees the motes, they remind him of the cloud in Las Vegas, of the painter's wife and the hospital, of Linda. His neck and face well with shame. He turns to the digging, to the mindless work to forget.

At the start of the day, Joe introduces Guillermo and Manny to Nolan as:

—Los Hermanos de Zacatecas.

The Brothers from Zacatecas.

Guillermo is the older and more serious of the two, while Manuel, a tall, skinny, handsome trickster, is in his late twenties. Manny has been working for Joe for only several months, but Guillermo has been with the contractor for over fifteen years.

—Picked him up the day I got my license, Joe tells Nolan at lunch that first day.

The Mexican was seventeen years old then, barrel-chested and broad-shouldered and already a skilled carpenter.

—Dude won this strongman competition down in Zaca. People stream down from the hills and everybody lifts cats and dogs and shit. Old people even get in on it, lifting, like, lizards and mice.

Nolan and Joe sit in the shade on the front porch of the farmhouse near Manny, while Guillermo sits off by himself with his eyes closed, resting against a cut two-by-ten. In a large field below the farmhouse a swath of chamomile runs across the carpet of grasses, grasses already losing their green beneath the heat of the spring sun.

—But it all comes down to two or three hombres who can lift a pig, Joe says. Billy-boy here won by raising a donkey.

Joe lifts his chin in the Mexican's direction.

—Dude lifted a burro off the ground, bro. Think about that.

On that first day Nolan learns that Joe, who is in his late forties, is married to a woman who has a teenage daughter and that he and his wife have a young son, named Joey. Joe tells Nolan he was born and raised in San Clemente, an ocean-side city just south of Los Angeles, and that he spent his formative years surfing the coastline of southern California and Baja California Norte and Sur. He arrived in Burnridge when he was twenty years old at the helm of a German-made van he steered with a broken arm after having attempted to surf the cold tsunami waves of Mavericks.

—When my wave came up and I dropped in, I saw the whole thing flash before my eyes, bro, just all of it. All I remember is waking up on the beach, people all around me, blue sky. Something stilled in me that day, and ever since then, life's been nothing but perfect, empty sets.

At the end of the first day, Joe offers Nolan a month of demolition and salvage work, and if things work out, the journeyman may be able to stay on for the duration of the remodel as the second low man.

—I should have enough work until the end of summer, mid-fall at the latest.

But, that first day on the job, Joe also makes it clear that, despite Nolan's experience, he will report to Guillermo, the site's foreman.

—You need to understand, bro, Guillermo's my boy. You may have skills, and we may speak the same *lengua*, but Billy-boy and me, we go back deep time.

—I'm just grateful for the work, sir.

—Don't call me, sir, bro. No hierarchies, all right?

—I apologize.

—No worries, just don't do it anymore.

Nolan falls easily into the rhythms of work again. He slips into the days, all while picking up gradually on the details that make the place what it was, what it is, what it's becoming.

On his second day he unearths a blue glass canning jar, several old medicine bottles, and a set of brass hinges; on his third day, when Guillermo and Joe are off site on a side job, he inspects the foreman's layout and cuts and has nothing but respect for the carpenter; after work on Thursday, Joe invites Nolan over to the truck for a beer after Manny and Guillermo leave and the two men look over the blueprints to the remodel, spread out over the hood of Joe's Ram, and Nolan can feel Joe sussing out his knowledge with pointed questions.

But during that first week, Nolan spends the bulk of his time with Manny, and in that time he learns that Manny can talk. He learns that all of the men in Manny and Guillermo's family, except for their father, are working in California, participants in one of the world's great diasporas, and that before coming to work for Joe, Manny was on the floor of a cola factory in St Louis, Missouri. Nolan learns that Manny dislikes the abundance of sugar in American cuisine, that he's been drunk only once in his life, and that he harbors a fondness that borders on fetish for a select few classic American automobiles.

—*El Mustang*, he whistles, pushing his index finger against his thumb and shaking down and loose the bottom three fingers of his right hand, two, three times, chest high. Mustang is the best.

As low men, Manny and Nolan are assigned the rudimentary apprentice work essential to the farmhouse remodel. They dig the footings for the new piers and stem walls; they unload, haul, and mix the concrete sacks in the tight, cramped space beneath the floor joists; they tear out the double-hung windows and rip down the sheetrock and the fiberglass insulation from the walls; they salvage the antique hardware from all the doors and light switches and all the kitchen and bathroom cabinets; they make the dump runs. It's dirty, strenuous work, made easy by conversation.

—You have wife? Manny asks Nolan on Monday morning of Nolan's second week on the job.

—Nope.

—Girlfriend?

—Nope.

—You *joto*?

—Nope.

—Ah, Manuela.

Manny is twenty-nine, Nolan learns. He's been married for four years already to a woman ten years his junior, and in the moment of silence it takes for Nolan to do the math on that one, he can feel Manny grinning at him a grin that in the English language is best described as shit-eating.

—You mean to say she—

—*No, está OK*. Manny smiles. *En México*, when he, the father, when he write the paper, *no hay problema*.

—No problemo, huh?

—*Sí*, no problem.

Manny and his child bride and their three-year-old daughter, a little girl whose name translates into English as star, live in a two-bedroom apartment they share with Guillermo, who has no women in his life, or none that Manny speaks of if he knows. Manny is the youngest of the five brothers, all of whom work in construction, the trade their father taught them, and their father's father, him. But Manny's dream is to own a chain of car washes in Zacatecas, a major metropolitan area two hours north of the pueblo where he and Guillermo were born and raised.

—Cha-ching, Joe tries to teach Manny how to say at lunch one day.

—Ching-ching.

—No. Cha. Cha.

—Chan-ching.

—Forget it, Joe says.

But for as much as Nolan gets along with Manny and Joe during those first two weeks, he feels a quiet, steady tension between him and Guillermo. They're roughly the same age and approximate in skill. Every now and then, when Joe asks Nolan for his take on a situation, Nolan senses a change in Guillermo's presence, a defensiveness, as if he's wary of the ease of communication between Joe and Nolan and bitter at Manny's effort to learn English and Nolan's to learn Spanish. For all his years working and living in the United States, Guillermo's English is rudimentary at best, his vocabulary limited to his trade.

—Maybe you and Joe have work *en el futuro*, Manny says to Nolan one afternoon while Joe and Guillermo are out on a lumber run. Maybe you and Joe no need Los Hermanos.

—I'm a short-timer here, Manny.

—*¿Cómo?*

—I no work here *mucho tiempo*.

—*¿Por qué no?*

—*Porque no vivo aquí.*

—Where you live?

—Here and there.

—*Es imposible.* Live here and there.

—It's a figure of speech, Manny.

—*¿Cómo?*

—Never mind.

One morning during Nolan's second week, the four of them stand on the farmhouse porch to watch a half dozen hot-air balloons, their baskets filled with tourists, rise up through the fog hovering above the valley floor in the shadow of Fumarole Peak. The colorful patterns of the balloons stand out against the mountain, tall and majestic and covered in grasses drying to a tawny-drab beneath the lingering sun. Hillsides the color of the deer that cross them. The builders listen to the tourists chatter, the stillness of the valley punctuated by their voices and by bursts of flaming gas from the balloons.

The last of the balloons are still in the air when the crew stops for an early lunch. While Guillermo dozes off to the side against his plank, in a large plastic mug Manny mixes a can of tuna fish, a plastic baggie of canned corn, chopped jalapeño, and two single-serving-size packets of mayonnaise. Nolan eats a smoked turkey sandwich on wheat bread, and Joe fashions bites of sautéed kale, brown rice, and baked tempeh from a wooden bowl using a pair of stainless steel chopsticks. Raising the bowl to his face and stuffing his mouth, he says to Nolan:

—You know, man, you ever need a lift, just say the word.

—I appreciate that, but I enjoy the ride.

Manny quietly scoops the tuna salad onto salty soda crackers and douses the combination with hot sauce. Chewing, he watches the balloons between bites.

—How do you like living in Valley Oaks? Joe asks.

—I like it just fine.

—Place went up overnight.

—About how tracts do.

—When I first landed here, Valley Oaks was all prune orchards, not even grapes, yet. I used to take ladies out there when the trees were in bloom. We'd bring a blanket and a fat doobie and snuggle up and trip out on all the petals drifting down like snowflakes. Man, they dug that. Mother nature will get you laid every time, bro.

Guillermo begins to snore, and Manny raises an eyebrow and smiles mischievously. He gets to his feet, creeps over, and crumbles a cracker all over Guillermo's chest.

Joe says:

—Let sleeping dogs lie, Manny.

—*¿Cómo?*

—*Perro durmiendo.*

—No, Manny says, sitting back down, *perrito*.

Joe chopsticks kale into his mouth and says to Nolan:

—You apprentice on tracts?

—I did.

—Just a bunch of dudes building their muscles and working on their tans.

—I heard that said on a rooftop in Texas once.

—What about, can't see it from my house?

—Heard that here in California.

—Ain't no Steinway?

—New Mexico.

—Good enough for government work?

—Nevada.

—Good enough for the girls we go with?

—Oregon.

—Damn, bro, you been around.

Nolan nods.

—I worked this one tract, Joe says around the food in his mouth, Rancho something or other, down out of Bakersfield. The foreman there would show up every Friday at quitting time with two shoeboxes full of cash and, I shit you not, the bed of his El Camino filled with crushed ice and cold beer. I don't know how many journeymen were on that tract, but we'd grab a couple two, three beers, get in line and he'd pay us out. Five o'clock rolls around at the end of a hot summer Friday, and up rolls this El Camino filled with cold beer. Easily the best summer of my life. Partied like a rock star.

Joe sets the chopsticks in the bowl and wipes his mouth on the back of his sleeve. Then, he reaches up under his serape and produces a package of rolling tobacco.

—Young bucks nowdays, they *no comprendes*, bro. None of them ever had to work tracts. Tracts around here are all Mexicans with nail guns. All the lily-white boys around here, all they know is high-end, boom shit. Finish work and jobs with architects on site. Restoration remodels and eight, nine, ten-thousand-square-foot custom jobbies. Real magazine-quality, yuppie shit. Bunch of bucks all covered in tats like they've done time, throwing paychecks at gas-powered toys like it'll never end. Bragging about buddies they got in Iraq, Afghanistan, like their spending habits aren't part of the equation. Shit. They've never had to weather the lean years, never had to hustle up some work. They don't remember '91. Hell, you probably don't remember '91.

—I caught the tail end of it.

—Tail end was the rebound.

Nolan nods.

—Ups and downs, man, and we're due for a down. Mark it.

Joe gestures over to where Manny sits cleaning the inside of his mug with a tortilla.

—Meanwhile, Billy and Manny here fret about getting sent back down south. Fucking builders of civilization and they got to be worried about getting deported. Fucking astonishes the reasonable mind.

The final balloon descends to the valley floor, and a passenger van with tinted windows drives across the field to meet it, leaving dark, parallel tracks across the chamomile.

—The other day, Joe continues, I heard about this one job, down by the plaza here, this old Victorian. They got half a dozen carpenters for an entire year's worth of finish work. Can you believe that? A year's worth.

Joe fingers tobacco into the channel of paper and then takes from the sack a plastic baggie rolled over a length of crushed marijuana.

—But, bro, you hear about tracts going up down around Phoenix, Santa Fe, Vegas, tracts like five, six times the size of Valley Oaks, all these retirement communities built on golf courses out in the middle of the desert. Real common-sense-type shit. Dudes working under flood lights at night it's so hot.

—I know it firsthand.

—So, you know, man. You know.

The van parks and the tourists who have climbed out of

the balloon's basket are standing off to the side. A few of them take pictures of the balloon folding in on itself.

—A few years back, I land this project two blocks from the plaza. Sweet little craftsman bungalow this couple from the city bought. Tony and Toni. True story.

Joe raises the spliff, licks the tacky edge of the rolling paper, and expertly folds it over itself before twisting one end gently.

—Me and Billy drop anchor on the place. Time and material up the wazoo. The husband's this doctor on some reality television show. Swear to dog. *Inner-city ER*, or some shit like that. She's in on this start-up in Silicon Valley. Oodles of tech money. Kind that survived the dot-com bubble, no problem. They're of the beautiful people. Double income, no kids. Train for triathlons together. Do yoga. Get colonics. You can hear the sex from miles away.

Nolan watches the balloon splay out over the field, nearly deflated, colorful folds sagging into colorful folds. Manny takes out a flip-phone and begins texting.

—Anyway, it takes me and Billy-boy a year and a half to finish. I hand over change-order after change-order, and the Tonys, they don't flinch. Not once. Never.

—Nice.

—No doubt, right? But then they move in.

—Here we go.

—But it's not what you think. Our work's tight. Billy's a stud. I'm a carpenter Titan. But the pool, man, brand-new in-ground swimming pool that runs north–south. Every time the doctor swims laps, the sun's in his eyes when he goes to breathe. So they tear out the pool and put in a brand-new one that runs east–west.

Joe tucks the baggie of weed into the cigarette pouch

and reaches under his serape and puts the pouch away. Nolan watches as he places the spliff at the corner of his mouth and raises a plastic lighter to the end of it, the flame tiny and blue. Exhaling smoke, Joe says:

—Fucking people like that, it's no wonder some dude's running around here trying to burn all the old houses to the ground.

6

Saturday morning. Nolan wakes at six but stays on the love seat in the garage, wrestling with a headful of thoughts until seven. After cooking a leisurely breakfast of cheesy eggs, seasoned home fries, and uncured bacon, he borrows Cosmo's Valiant so that by nine he is at the hardware store spending part of his first paycheck on a hammer, framing square, and tape. By 9:30 he is outside the opening doors of the one local workwear shop, where he buys underwear, socks, two work shirts, and a new pair of blue jeans. At the local nursery, a mile south of town, he picks up several bags of soil amendment for the raised garden beds, along with tomato, basil, pepper, kale, squash, and arugula starts. On the drive back to Valley Oaks, he stops at a high-end grocery store and buys chicken thighs, which marinate in lemon, red wine vinegar, oregano, and rosemary while Nolan spends the afternoon working the soil and arranging and planting the vegetable garden.

That evening, with the light golden in the canopy hollows of a neighbor's oak, the chicken thighs hiss on the grill and Nolan, freshly showered and standing barefoot on the concrete patio in his new jeans and a long-sleeved denim button-up he bought his first week in Burnridge at the Goodwill, looks over his day's work while dribbling beer now and then on flames fueled by the dripping chicken fat, but careful with the dribbling so as to avoid raising soot. It's a peaceful, comfortable summer evening in the first week of May, a backyard evening scented by a neighbor's jasmine and fabric softener. Clothes dryers run and automated watering systems switch on. Cooking sounds and snippets of conversation, both real and televised, reach the backyard.

Cosmo, sitting nearby, leans back in his chair and exhales marijuana smoke at the sky. He adjusts his eyeglasses as the breeze shifts and smoke from the barbeque gets in his eyes.

—It doesn't get much better than this, he says, slouching back and resting his forearm on the top of his head. Life in the *contado*.

—I don't know that word, Nolan says, sitting in the lawn chair opposite Cosmo.

—The *contado* is the area beyond the city that sustains and enriches the city. They cut down our trees, mine our hills, and divert our water, for which the city provides protection and some sense of luxury. It's kind of like benevolent pillaging.

Cosmo scoots forward in the seat:

—Did you know that for the first time in recorded history, the population of humans in urban areas has surpassed the population of rural areas?

—Can't say I did.

—Historians and scientists believe we're living at the end of the Agrarian Age. They say this is a new geological epoch because we've altered the Earth so much. Did you know that?

—I didn't.

—The Anthropocene. And you and I, we keep the entire thing interconnected.

—How's that?

—I write sentences, you drive nails, and together we bask in the spoils of war and assist in the fabrication of this vast and expanding network of interconnectivity. Believe it or not, us two, sitting here, this is us assisting in the war effort.

Cosmo drops his joint to the concrete and steps on it with the toe of his scuffed Hush Puppy.

—Did you know hospitals are introducing robot doctors? Not, like, cyborgs, but these four-foot-tall robots with screens and cameras.

—No, I didn't.

—Yeah, they're like these robots with screens for faces that wheel around hospitals.

Nolan stands and turns the chicken on the grill. Grease hisses on the flames. Cosmo says:

—Not everyone is OK with this, you understand.

—No, I get it.

—I mean, think about this, are we prepared for this level of disassociation of the body and mind? What does this mean for us as a species? In the long run?

All of a sudden, loud, discordant music plays from backyard speakers located several houses down the block on their side of the street. Somehow, Nolan knows the music comes from a house where, in his first two weeks at Cosmo's, he has seen and heard a middle-aged woman and her teenage daughter come and go separately or argue loudly. The aggressive drumming, inarticulate bass, and mashed guitar sounds alter the weekend tranquility of the housing tract in the same way the mother and daughter's frequent arguments have startled him with their sharpness and meanness. Sitting up and looking in the direction of the noise, Cosmo raises his voice while continuing:

—They say we're connected like a web, but that's just the shape for now. In the future, like, way in the future, we'll learn it looks nothing like a web. It'll be like nothing we know now because we'll model it on something we know then. It's the same way we no longer think of time as an arrow or a sundial.

—What do you think it will look like?

—I don't know, but I think if we ever figure it out, the light bulbs will explode in our domes and we, as we know we, this, this will be gone lickety-split.

Cosmo stands, adjusts his pants, and stretches his back.

—Have you ever considered your part in all this? he asks Nolan. You know, what your hands have done?

—I have.

—And?

—I feel like I'm a small part of something big.

Cosmo walks to the fence line, in the direction of the music, and stands on the edge of the raised garden bed and peers over the fence.

—Do you ever wonder where's it all going? he asks Nolan. Have you thought about that?

—It's just what we do.

—What about when we're gone?

—We're gone.

—And that doesn't bother you? Scare you?

—There's not much I can do about it.

—Bullshit, Cosmo says, jumping down from the raised bed. You, me, we're complicit in the destruction.

—I like to think of myself as a builder.

—So you're a lover, not a fighter.

—That's not what I said.

—It doesn't matter what you say, you take material from

the earth and shape it into something else. I do the same thing, just with the abstract. And we—Cosmo points at Nolan and then at his own chest—we done over-built, partner. Put the blame where the blame is due. No one, and I mean no one, is innocent. We are all complicit because we impose order upon matter just as matter imposes order on us. Matter is all that is, and peace is stasis, and stasis is death. But why do I care? Why do I think about it? Because of my geospatial location and the socioeconomic factors that shape this place? Because of the vocabulary of my environment? Because my father suffered from PTSD before there was a PTSD from which to suffer?

Nolan looks down into the mouth of his beer. A garbled voice begins to sing above the music, words Nolan can't extract from the wall of sound.

—Our enemy, Cosmo says while rolling his shoulders and then pulling his arm across his chest by cupping his elbow, our enemy believes we as a nation have reached a stage of effeminacy. They write this, declare it to one another in writing and on web videos as an assessment of how best to end us. Them pussies are all words, they say. Labial, dental, guttural. Ductile, malleable, sectile.

Cosmo raises his index finger and wags it at Nolan.

—But the arsonist, he gets it *and* he's got the cojones to do something about it. He lights fires to clear out the understory so it can grow back stronger.

Cosmo abruptly leans over, picks up his bottle of beer, turns it over, and shakes out the last bit as he takes the few steps toward the kitchen's screened door. Nolan watches him, sensing somehow that his brother has decided how he wants to respond to the music. With a hand on the door's handle, Cosmo points at Nolan's beer and asks:

—You want another?

—Please.

While Cosmo is inside, Nolan stands and turns the meat on the grill and again he pours a small amount of beer on the flames to knock them down. He can hear Cosmo inside, rooting around the refrigerator. For some reason, it makes him think of one night when Nolan was still in high school after Cosmo had gone off to Cal. Nolan came home late to find their father sitting on the living-room couch, in front of the television, watching the 10 o'clock news. He always sat in the middle of the couch when he was alone, in the middle of the couch and straight backed, with his hands palms down on his thighs, as if he were meditating. How many times did Nolan find him like this, tired at the end of a long day at work, following events around the world that he claimed direct connection to, that he claimed some special purchase on because of the events of his youth?

But this time was different. Nolan took off his shoes and jacket at the door, greeted his father, who greeted him back, and he walked into the kitchen and opened the fridge door and stood in the cold bright light, debating his choices. He heard his father change the channel from the news to a comedian's late-night talk show. The comedian's voice diligently working its way through a scripted monologue, during which Nolan's father laughed, lightly at first, and then loudly, genuinely, with the comedian's voice rising to be heard above the studio audience's rising laughter and applause. Nolan heard the show transition to a commercial. His father continued laughing, but there was something odd about his laughter that compelled Nolan to check on him. He found his father crying. A grown man, on a couch before a television, late at night in his own home, sitting still as tears streamed down his face. Nolan walked into the room and placed his hand on his father's shoulder.

—You all right, Dad?

—No, his father said, placing his hand on Nolan's but not taking his eyes from the television. Let me be alone, bud, OK?

In Cosmo's backyard, Nolan stares at the barbeque coals. Orange-red scrims of ember oscillate along thin lines of white ash.

Effeminacy?

From the kitchen, Cosmo says:

—How come we never go out and meet any women?

Nolan looks up at the marine layer absorbing the light of the small town, and says:

—Because you're a mess.

—What's that?

—I said, let's do it.

Cosmo returns with a fresh joint at the corner of his mouth, two cold beers, and a full carton of free range, antibiotic-free, vegetarian-fed eggs that Nolan bought that morning when buying the chicken and some fresh salad greens. Food like his brother hadn't eaten in how long? Food the likes of which he would eat how often after Nolan had gone? Cosmo hands Nolan a beer and then sets the carton of eggs on his chair.

—If you're about to do what I think you're about to do, Nolan says to Cosmo, don't.

—Are you your brother's keeper?

—For one, I paid for those and that's not how I want them used, and two, it's not right.

—Right is relative.

—Have you seen the lady who lives there? That's a single mom down there.

—She's not a single mom.

—How do you know?

—Because I pay attention to these types of things. I listen to their arguments. It's a house divided, and the father is currently in absentia. Besides, Cosmo says as he opens the carton and pulls out a single egg, my beef isn't with the parental units. My beef is with their hellion offspring.

—Cos, Nolan says, but Cosmo tucks the joint behind his ear, licks a finger, raises it to gauge some imaginary wind, and, before throwing the egg at the noise, he says:

—Stir the web, wake the spider.

Several days later, on his way home from work Nolan notices a telephone booth as he rides past the Chinese restaurant at the north end of town. The aluminum frame rectangle stands tall and empty, its glass windows covered with pollen and dust. Without hesitation, he swings the bicycle around, buys a prepaid calling card at the gas station quick mart across the street, ducks into the phone booth, and dials the numbers, hesitating briefly before the last one, but finally pushing it through.

Linda answers on the third ring:

—Hello.

—Hey, Nolan says.

A dense quiet coalesces at the other end of the connection. The receiver feels sticky against his ear.

—What do you want, Nolan?

—I just wanted see how you are. To hear your voice.

—I'm fine.

—Good.

In the background, children playing in the community pool. She must be walking toward the bedroom window, or sitting at the foot of her bed, facing the window, the comforter pulled taut and extra pillows heaped at the headboard.

—A letter, Nolan?

—I know.

—No, obviously you don't.

—Yeah.

—I didn't think I was wrong about you. I thought you were a good guy.

—Yeah.

—Yeah? she scoffs. All you have to say is, "yeah"?

Frustrated, he lowers his forehead against the glass, tipping his hat back on his head. A jeep pulls into the restaurant's parking lot and noses within feet of the phone booth. Bland faces within the vehicle turn their eyes on him, sudden audience to his misery.

—I want you to leave me alone, Nolan.

—I'm sorry, Linda.

—Me, too. I wish you didn't think it was OK to just run like that.

—I know.

—No, you don't. Not yet, you don't.

He sits on the love seat, drinking beer alone in the garage with the front door up and the side door open in hopes of cooling the room still hot from a day when the heat was enough to stave off the coming of the marine layer. Air conditioners hum alongside the houses, and children, out of school and out of doors, ride bicycles and scooters up and down the long block.

Work under the farmhouse has been especially hot during his fourth week, and Nolan still feels it after a cold shower and several cold beers. A cool breeze comes up the sloped driveway off the shaded street, but still his face and neck are hot, and some of that, he realizes, is the shame that lingers from his conversation with Linda.

He could tell from the tone of her voice and the length of her silences that he'd hurt her.

—Duh, she'd said pointedly to him a time or two when he'd stated the obvious. Duh or No, duh, and always with eyes acknowledging she knew other words, longer words, but that those words, in this case, worked weakly, and he was to understand that.

He sits oiling the snub-nosed .38, a gift from his father on the day he set out with the Airstream at nineteen.

—You know what this is? his father asked him, looking him forcefully in the eye.

—Yes, sir.

—You know what it's for?

—I do.

—Good. Be smart with it. Don't be careless or stupid. Owning one's a privilege, not a right.

Nolan wipes the soot clean from the fireproof box and while doing so he considers selling the handgun for cash and using the money to buy a bus ticket back to Vegas, to work there instead of Burnridge, to build his stake and try to reconnect with Linda. He wonders how many times she would close the door on him before finally opening it. Could he wait that out? Then, why leave in the first place?

—You're quiet, she said once after they'd been kissing. She took off his hat and put it on her own head and they kissed, pressing their bodies against one another and smoothing and grabbing at one another, and during a calm to catch their breaths she put the hat back on his head, and straightening it she said, You're quiet, but you do have a flare for the dramatic.

Cosmo is in his office again with the door closed, typing. Nolan wipes the revolver's blued metal free of his fingerprints and slides five shiny brass cartridges into their chambers, feeling at his fingertips how the cylinder fits the machined rest with a soft click, so seamless and smooth, the simple result of millennia of tinkering.

With the handgun loaded, Nolan aims it at the cardboard box in front of him, his finger pointed along the cylinder, nowhere near the trigger.

—Pow, he says quietly.

As he lowers the gun, he notices that several of the boxes have been opened and Cosmo's rooted through them. He can see the carving platter he gave Cosmo and Dawn as a gift and it makes Nolan wonder whether his brother was searching through the boxes for something in particular or just revisiting items from his marriage. Nolan can imagine him doing this, eyes bleary from alcohol and weed, hair greasy and disheveled, angry and sad all at once.

There have been several times since Nolan moved in with Cosmo that he's considered mentioning his brother's marriage and divorce, but each time he edged away from doing so because talk like that is not something they've done, it's not something they did when their father was diagnosed with lung cancer, when he was dying. After Nolan's mother told him over the phone of the diagnosis, she asked him to call Cosmo because he'd taken it hard. Then, she put his father on, and he said:

—Yeah, can't say we didn't see this one coming.

After talking with his father, Nolan didn't call Cosmo, and Cosmo didn't call him.

At the end, pneumonia set in. Their father died quickly and peacefully, during the night's false dawn. Cosmo was home and he and their mother were at the bedside. Nolan was on an interstate, driving home. Dash lights and the reflectors in the road before him. Choking back tears, thinking, I do not want to see you die. I will see you dead.

Cosmo was silently furious with Nolan when he finally arrived, later that morning. Even then, his brother was already an amateur alcoholic. Not yet the stoner, though. On Nolan's walk down the hallway to see his father's corpse, Cosmo shouldered him and hissed:

—Selfish prick.

The sound of his car spinning in the gravel driveway as he drove away for most of the day while Nolan held vigil with his mother. His father's stillness concentrated between them.

—The first time I brought him home, your grandmother said, "You always did have a soft spot for injured angels."

Late that afternoon, the funeral home came to take him and Nolan and Cosmo helped as two young men lifted the sheeted cart into the back of the hearse. They spent a week with their mother, not talking much to one another, listening to and comforting her. Cosmo was the first to leave. They stood on the porch as he drove away.

—He's not wrong, Nolan, she said once Cosmo was gone. You could have made more of an effort to be here sooner.

—I'm sorry.

—I'm not the one you should be apologizing to.

Nolan thought she meant his father, but months later, while sitting on a rock in the middle of a mountain lake, watching swallows slice back and forth through a scrim of gnats gathered above the water, he realized she had meant Chance. Cosmo. Brothers both.

Truth be told, though, Nolan doesn't know Cosmo all that well. He didn't want to come for the wedding because, from all he'd heard from his mother, he believed the marriage wouldn't last, and what's the point of taking time off from a steady paycheck just to watch your messed-up older brother marry a woman you suspect will leave him because they're too young to know any better and too arrogant to try?

He doesn't know Cosmo, but he does. In Nolan's first month in Burnridge, his brother's fascination with the arsonist has blossomed into an obsession. According to Cosmo, pressure is mounting on local officials to stop the arsons before tourism is affected, before something other than old, abandoned houses get destroyed.

—Before it becomes the main attraction, as Cosmo says.

Although Nolan won't say it, he is worried about his brother. One night Nolan got up to urinate and he found Cosmo asleep in front of the television, bathed in the blue glow, reeking of wood and synthetics smoke, as if he'd been poking around the scene of the crime, spending time among the charred ruins.

The video-game controller was upside down in his lap, and looped music played as Cosmo's female avatar stood in an open meadow, turning from side to side, alert but waiting, scantily clad and disproportionate and armed with a recurve bow. Abruptly, the avatar took several steps and then stopped. She nocked an arrow, drew back the string as if to shoot, and then lowered the bow and turned from side to side before returning to her original position.

—Default mode, Cosmo called it, suddenly awake. She's operating in default mode.

The light of the television changed as the avatar moved, and out of the corner of his eye Nolan noticed their father's copper Zippo, tucked in Cosmo's shirt pocket.

—You all right? Cosmo asked.

—Yeah. You?

—Golden.

He didn't think Chance was capable of setting fires like the ones that had been set, but he didn't know if Cosmo was. He knew their father had given Cosmo the lighter same as he'd given Nolan the gun, but Nolan didn't know what the man had said to Cosmo, he didn't know how Cosmo had responded, or what was in his eyes when he did. They had their own moments with their father, and about those they had spoken little, if at all.

A car passes along the street, bringing Nolan back to the garage. He takes a sip of his beer, empties the .38 cartridges into his shirt pocket, takes another sip of the beer, and thumbs the hammer back on the revolver. He dry fires the handgun once at the box in front of him, stands, and lifts the flap on one of the cardboard moving boxes. At the top of the box he finds a picture of Cosmo and his wife standing on a beach in Baja California Sur. Their honeymoon. A hotel looms in the near distance and a crescent-shaped beach curves around the gently lapping waters of a calm bay. The word *Canción* reads across the bottom of the photo. Song.

Suddenly, bellowing thumps of a steady bass line increase in volume until a raised, four-wheel-drive mini-Ranger lurches onto the quiet street, speeding recklessly, loud noise blasting from speakers in the bed of the truck. Nolan looks up from the photo, sets it back in the box, and walks out of the garage and down the driveway, tucking the handgun in the waist of his blue jeans at the small of his back.

He's halfway down the sloped driveway when Cosmo sprints past, dressed in his bathrobe and slippers. Cosmo stumbles at the end of the driveway, loses a slipper, kicks off the other, and continues barefoot toward where the truck parks in front of the house down the way.

—Cosmo, Nolan calls after, but his voice is lost in the blaring music.

As the truck is pulling up in front of the house, the front door opens and the teenage girl Nolan has seen come and go runs from the house and down the driveway, followed by her mother.

—Hey, sweetheart, Cosmo yells at the girl. Hey, who do you think you are?

When the girl gets to the bottom of the driveway, the passenger-side door to the truck opens from inside and the girl hops up and in. The truck lurches forward as she pulls the door shut behind her. Defeated, the mother stops at the top of the driveway. Her shoulders slouch.

Cosmo stops as the truck speeds to the end of the street before whipping back around, lolling on its leaves. With the mini-Ranger approaching, Cosmo stands defiantly at the side of the street, his bathrobe open at the top, his bare feet planted on the hot pavement, his fists on his hips, and a shock of hair shoved upright in a suggestion of cultivated mania.

The music carves out space for itself in the suburban calm, it bores through the quiet, and as the truck passes Cosmo, the girl leans across the young man driving and with her young, pretty, excessively made-up face contorted into a hideous mask, she raises her middle finger and sticks out her tongue.

Cosmo stands there astonished for a second or two after they're gone, the bass fading. Then, he ties the belt of his robe around his waist and walks back to the house. Nolan looks to where the mother was standing but she is gone and the front door to the house is closed. He can still feel the bass in his lungs long after the truck has made its way out to Burnridge Avenue. When Cosmo walks within reach, Nolan places his hand on his brother's shoulder.

—There's nothing you can say to that, Cosmo says, his glasses crooked and his jaw muscles clenching and unclenching.

—Come back inside, Cos.

—Absolutely nothing that will make her understand her role in the coarsening of our society, in the downfall of our republic.

—Let's drink a cold beer, bud.

7

After shoring the foundation, Manny and Nolan set about gutting the house clean. They rip out stained carpet and padding in the bedrooms and they pry yellowed asbestos tiles from the kitchen floor. Tearing down the living-room sheetrock, they find wallpaper so brittle it crumbles into a fibrous dust in the palm of their gloved hands and swirls before their masked faces. Behind the wallpaper run redwood lath boards a true foot wide. Beautiful old wood.

The low men pull wiring hand over fist and toss porcelain insulators out gaping holes where double-hung windows once stood. They yank free heavy quilts of chipped tile and sawzall rusted galvanized water pipes from the second-story bathroom. They walk through rooms sunshot and roiling with motes as they haul moldy swaths of fiberglass down the stairs and out the back door, leaving drag marks through the farmhouse in the sheetrock and wallpaper dust. In one day alone they amass a garbage heap in the driveway nearly a story tall.

Joe meets them at the end of that day with a Mexican beer and lime for Nolan and a cola for Manny.

—A lot of trash, he says to Nolan, handing the journeyman the beer.

—Yes, it is.

They all three stand looking over the trash heap.

—One day, Joe says, all that was new.

—*No más,* Manny says.

—That's what I just said, Manny. *No más.*

—*Sí, no más.*

—Always have to have the last word, don't you, smartass?

—*¿Cómo?* Manny smiles, sipping his cola.

—*Cómo,* my ass, Joe says. You know what I meant.

It's moments like these that leave Nolan feeling most at ease in Burnridge. He likes the camaraderie, the talk, the harmless practical jokes Manny plays on Guillermo and Joe. He also likes spending eight to ten hours of his day being held accountable for things he can handle. The tasks at hand focus his mind and keep at bay the troubles that hound him when he's off work. On the ride to the farmhouse, he goes over in his mind the day's jobs. As a low man with a journeyman's experience, it's difficult to get too excited about the work, but it reminds him of simple things he'd forgotten—how to use a shovel efficiently, how to mix quick-setting concrete effectively, how to use your body judiciously in backbreaking work.

Each morning, Manny and Joe flip a coin to determine the station to which the radio will be tuned until lunch. Joe favors classic rock to the local Spanish-language channel Manny always chooses. Nolan and Guillermo don't care either way. When Joe wins, he lowers his head and nods while raising his right hand, index finger and pinkie splayed, thumb pressing down the middle two fingers to form Satan's horns.

—Yeah, baby, he says. Rock 'n' roll, baby.

To which Manny responds by turning down the corners of his mouth and raising his shoulders in a shrug.

But when Manny wins, he bends back at the waist and raises his hands before his face to play a triumphant air trombone out of the corner of his mouth while Joe covers his ears and groans.

Nolan enjoys listening to the Spanish-language station. He pays attention to the lyrics, picking out the words he recognizes so as to translate them and to contrive some semblance of a story. Each day that summer he hears the story about the man who bears 1,000 scars from love, that and the story that begins with the father making a long-distance call home to Mexico to talk with his wife and his son.

—This guy, Manny says one afternoon while standing on a ladder to pull insulation from the ceiling and handing it to Nolan, who stuffs the lengths into heavy-gauge trash sacks. This guy is *no más.*

—*No más, no más?* Nolan asks.

—*Sí,* Manny says, dragging his thumb across his throat. *Drogas.*

—Oh.

—You know *drogas?*

—I do.

—You like?

—Not really.

—You know cartel?

—Just from the newspapers.

—Is crazy in Mexico.

—I read that.

—This one time, I see a man stop his car and put a man from his trunk, you know? Manny says, miming dragging a corpse from the trunk of a vehicle. This man is *muerto.*

—A dead man.

—You know this? *Muerto?*

—*Sí. Muerto.*

—Then this man, he take a gun and he shoot the man.

—The *hombre muerto?*

—*Sí.*

—*¿Por qué?*

—*Porque hay mucha* people in the street. He want the people to see him.

—Wow.

—Is crazy.

Most days, though, after listening to the Spanish-language station for an hour or less, Joe starts wailing from some far reach of the house and doesn't stop until he's made his way to the radio and changed the channel.

—*No más,* he screams. *No más tubas.*

Sometimes, he'll walk into the room where Nolan and Manny are working and cover his ears and yell over the music:

—*No más tubas,* Manny. Mañana, OK? I can't take it. I need my rock 'n' roll *clásico.* Mañana *tubas.* I promise.

—You promise? Manny says seriously.

—*Sí,* I promise.

—OK, mañana.

When Manny turns away, Joes says to Nolan:

—How can you stand that shit? It all sounds the same.

—He probably says the same thing about your music.

—My music? You mean our music?

—I mean classic rock.

—Did he say that?

—Say what?

—That it all sounds the same?

—Not that I know.

—I thought he might've said it to you in Spanish.

—My Spanish isn't that strong.

—You let me know if he does, though, all right?

—I'm not going to get mixed up in those games.

—Oh, it's too late for that, bro. You're committed to this site.

He is a house away from Cosmo's after a long day of work salvaging and cleaning hardware when, coasting the bicycle, he passes the teenage girl sitting in the green grass of her front yard between two teenage boys. All three have cigarettes in their hands and they sit in the shade of a crepe myrtle, just above where someone, using bleach, has written CONSERVE WATER in two-foot-tall letters across the width of the lawn.

The night before, Nolan was in the kitchen making white rice and a veggie stir-fry when Cosmo burst in smelling of beer and began complaining about how the teenager's lawn sprinklers were over-spraying the lawn and that water was puddling on the sidewalk. And this week after Cosmo had published a story in the *Observer* describing voluntary water-reduction measures suggested by the Burnridge city council.

—You know what this is? Cosmo said, pacing back and forth in the kitchen, an open beer in his hand.

—I'm sure you're going to tell me, Nolan said, tapping a wooden spoon on the edge of the wok he'd scored at the Salvation Army.

—We live in a disposable culture, Nolan. We drink water from disposable plastic bottles, we throw away our razor blades, we divorce our spouses.

—Grab a plate.

—How do they not see they're watering the sidewalk?

—I don't know.

—I do.

Extending a plate to Cosmo, Nolan looked deeply into his brother's eyes, alive with thoughts and thinking, and he didn't like what he saw there.

—They don't care, Cosmo said. Let others conserve while they water liberally.

As Nolan rides by the girl, she stares at him through a pair of dark sunglasses. Her painted lips a thin line, her jaw set.

—Bullet-proof vests burn worse than bullet-proof glass, one of the teenage boys says to the other.

—Like you know.

—That's what my cousin says. He says that shit straight-up ignites.

The young woman follows Nolan with her chin. She sits with her bare legs stretched out in front of her, a cigarette in her hand, and the smoke wafting above the shaded grass.

—Your cousin doesn't know shit.

—He bangs, yo.

—He ain't no gangsta.

—Say that to his face, fool.

—Fly his pranksta ass up here. I'll learn him how we roll.

Nolan looks away from the girl, but, seeing Cosmo's Valiant parked in the driveway ahead, he steps on the top pedal and pushes the bicycle forward.

He sets out on the bicycle for the hills west of town, for the cool of the windy back roads lined with maple and spice bush, for the rumpled and cracked asphalt roads dappled with sunlight and shadow. With the road to himself, he pedals and drifts, pedals and sways, allowing the momentum and the breeze to loosen thoughts free from his mind.

West of town, the road steepens severely. The road banks

are dense with poison oak and some of the buckeyes are in bloom. Nolan climbs off the ten-speed and pushes the bicycle up the hill. At the top of the incline, he notices a NO TRESPASSING sign. Beneath it, a well-trod footpath.

Nolan lingers by the edge of the road, checking in both directions and up the trail for game cameras. Then, he strikes out along the path and follows it up to the ridgeline. The dirt of the path is light as talc and he uses exposed roots as step treads. Spider webs gather on the insides of his elbows and he reads this to mean no one has been on the path for some time. He likes that; it satisfies something inside of him, something wordless and meaningful.

As he crests the ridgeline, a panoramic view of the river valley opens before him. Below, Burnridge lies nestled within a substantial crook in the river. He rests the bicycle against a fallen oak, which is also used as a makeshift bench, the bark on the tree worn smooth by people like him who come to sit and to watch and to listen.

It's an established town, Burnridge, a dream town cut off from the rest of the world by low hills studded with oaks. Glints of sunlight and motion lure Nolan's eye about the townscape, along streets shaded by a diversity of trees. He sits silently, listening carefully to his own breathing and then to the drone of bees in a nearby manzanita. The drone blends into the steady washes of highway traffic that reach him faintly from 101. He watches traffic on the highway bridge cross the river in opposite directions. From the bridge the river straightens and heads south, disappearing into a riparian line that divides the patchwork of green vineyards that extend as far as the eye can see, all that orderly green barely contained, it seems, by hills on both sides of the valley, wild oats gone golden and dry with summer and drought.

Down in the small town, sparks of light shine now and then, here and there, reflected off moving windshields. From the heritage homes to the postwar bungalows, the 1970s' farmhouses sided in T-111, and Valley Oaks Estates, in particular, where the trees have yet to mature, the rooflines resemble the tops of the walls of an intricate maze, an idea immured by milled wood, metal and asphalt, stucco, plastic, wire, and glass, a system of intercommunicating paths and passages.

—Don't you ever wonder where all the copper comes from? Cosmo asked Nolan the night before while they sat outside on the patio after eating the stir-fry, Cosmo calming some as he smoked his first joint of the night. Don't you wonder where all the wire that runs the stuff we leave on when no one's home comes from? We extract raw materials from the earth and convert them like acolytes to do our bidding.

Nolan scans the town below. He doesn't see what Cosmo sees, not all of it, and not because it's not there.

—Sometimes, Cosmo continued, blowing smoke over the cherry at the end of the joint, I think I can hear the telephone lines humming in the streets with all our mundane love songs and our caffeinated diatribes, our silences pregnant with meaning. I can hear and feel the matrix, held fast with nails and rebar. I'm attuned to the labyrinths of words hurrying us toward our collective ruin.

At the overlook, Nolan sits forward on the trunk bench and looks up at the sky, blue and cloudless. He closes his eyes. The air is hot and dry and still.

When he opens his eyes, he sees a head of smoke rising southeast of the plaza, not too far from the river. The smoke is black. A structure fire. And it lifts slowly and silently above the rooftops of the heritage homes and through the leafy canopy there.

—"To the man holding a hammer," Cosmo recited, "everything looks like a nail."

—That sounds like something someone who never picked up a hammer would say, Nolan responded.

—Maybe. Maybe not.

A siren calls from the fire station downtown. Then another siren, but from a different part of town, marked by a different pitch and whine. Both sirens hidden by trees and buildings. As the column of dense black smoke rises higher into the sky, beginning to redden along the ridgeline behind Nolan, the edges of the cloud become more clearly defined by the bluing of the sky to the east.

He wants to believe Chance didn't throw bleach on their neighbors' lawn. He wants to believe Chance would never go so far as to set houses to fire. He wants to believe these things, but the more time he spends with Cosmo, he just doesn't know.

When Nolan stands to leave, he notices a handful of unfiltered cigarette butts, crimpled white butts stubbed out in layers of boot prints. He looks away from the butts, grabs the handlebars of the bicycle, and does what he does whenever he's confronted with something he cannot fix, repair, or rebuild: he moves on.

Linda picks up on the third ring.

—Hello.

—Hey, it's Nolan.

Then, to fill the silence deepening at her end of the line, he says:

—How are you?

—I'm fine. What's up?

—I just wanted to hear your voice.

—Yeah, well, you should have treated me nicer.

—Linda.

—I'm where I need to be in my life, Nolan.

—Linda, listen.

—No, you listen. What the fuck is with you?

—Just hear me out.

—Really? Like I owe you that? Why is it that all the men I attract lately are, like, stuck in this malaise?

—Linda—

—This injured-little-boy malaise. Life is difficult, all right? It's challenging. Face it like a man.

Click.

That night he sits in Cosmo's backyard, looking up at the stars and steadily working his way through a twelve-pack of beer. Snatches of unintelligible conversation and loud music come from the house down the way. It sounds like the teenage girl has a few friends over and they're all gathered in her backyard.

Nolan came home to an empty house, despite Cosmo's Valiant parked in the driveway. Walking out to the patio, he stubbed his toe on the barbeque. Then, he hit his front tooth on the lip of his beer bottle and spilled most of that sip down the front of his shirt, which was clean. When he sat in one of the patio chairs, he heard the plastic supports crack like they might give.

—Go on and break, he said. Not like things can get any worse.

He sits there drinking for ten minutes by himself until a rustling sound stirs in the adjacent neighbor's yard, the fence dividing the properties shakes, and Cosmo tumbles over the fence and into the garden that Nolan so carefully planted in the raised bed. Cosmo stands, dusts himself off, and steps down onto the concrete patio.

—I was never here, he says with his index finger pressed to his thumb and three fingers raised to pass over Nolan a mind-erasing wave. You never saw me.

To which Nolan squints and says:

—Did you go through the other backyards to get there?

—Well, yeah, Cosmo says. Only a Jedi would dare to walk down the middle of the street.

—That wasn't smart.

—Actually, it was.

—If you got caught in one of those backyards—

—But if I was seen coming at them from the front, it would have ruined the element of surprise.

Nolan raises his hands and then drops them.

—I give up.

—There any more beer? Cosmo asks.

—Grab me another while you're at it.

Cosmo returns with two bottles of cold beer. He pulls the other chair nearer to Nolan and sits in it.

—There was another fire today, Cosmo says, taking his lighter from his shirt pocket.

—I saw the smoke.

—He went for it in broad daylight.

Cosmo uses his copper Zippo to lever the cap off one beer, which he hands to Nolan, and then the next, which he drinks from. Then, he settles back in the seat and produces from his coat pocket an empty bottle of organic fancy-grade maple syrup, which he sets on the concrete at the chair's leg.

—What's that all about? Nolan asks.

—Don't worry about it.

—If you did what I think you did—

—One, you have no idea what I did, and two, this is one of those situations where not knowing could keep you out of prison.

Nolan suppresses a smile.

—You ever think about walking down the street, knocking on the door, and talking all this out?

—Join hands and sing "Kumbaya"?

—Might work.

—No, it wouldn't, because they don't understand civility. In fact, I'd be willing to wager an everything-pizza dinner they can't even comprehend the possibility that they might be deserving of retaliation. Their field of comprehension doesn't reach that far.

Nolan laughs.

—What's so funny?

Nolan laughs again, but loudly, so Cosmo looks at him and states:

—You're drunk.

—Little bit. Nolan nods. Little bit.

—Tough day at the office?

—Just felt like getting drunk.

—On a school night?

—I don't have to be there until seven tomorrow.

—In that case, you want to smoke some weed?

—I might take a puff.

Cosmo produces a skinny joint from his shirt pocket and rolls it expertly between the ends of his fingers to straighten and to loosen it some before lighting the end with his Zippo.

—Got those things stashed all over your person, don't you?

—What was it Dad always said?

—Save me some ice cream?

—Prepare for the worst—

—And hope for the best.

Cosmo says:

—They're going to start filming the movie next week. They sent a copy of the screenplay to the newspaper so I can review it to get the locals to create buzz on social media.

—And?

—It's essentially a car commercial.

—What's the story?

Holding the smoke in his lungs, Cosmo says:

—You and story.

Nolan reaches for the joint and Cosmo hands it to him.

—It's about these two brothers who rob banks. The one brother's wife drives the getaway car. She's hot. They both want her. A love triangle ensues. It's one long, male-gaze-reinforcing chase scene. No way in hell it'll pass the Bechdel test.

—First part sounded like a good movie.

—It's a two-hour car commercial, Nolan.

Nolan takes a long drag on the joint and shrugs. He holds the smoke in his lungs until he coughs it up, and then he thrusts the joint back to Cosmo and takes a sip of his beer.

—That's all you want?

—All I need, Nolan says, wiping his mouth on the back of his hand to muffle his cough.

Relaxing in his chair, Cosmo smiles, satisfied. Then, he says:

—You remember when movies used to have generic products in them?

—No.

—Guy used to hold this white and blue can with BEER written on the side of it instead of some actual brand-name product.

—Can't say that I do.

—It's a shame they got rid of those. Fucking product placement ruined movies.

—There any product placements in that thing you're typing?

—Yeah, but I work my way around them.

Nolan wants to ask Cosmo about the bleach, but he feels the need to build to it. He hopes the weed doesn't make him forget.

—There really no story to it? he asks Cosmo.

—Of course there's a story to it.

—Let's hear it.

Cosmo sucks at his teeth and cracks his neck.

—I don't know.

—Come on. What else are we going to talk about?

—You're funny drunk.

—I'm funny, period.

—No.

—Says the Master of Comedy.

—Case in point.

—You're just pretentious.

—And you're not?

—How am I pretentious?

—Arugula and brie? Fresh pasta with buttered vegetables purchased from the farmers' market?

—That's just eating healthy.

—Healthily.

—See. Pretension.

—That's not pretension, Nolan. That's accuracy.

—Get to the story already.

Cosmo looks at the end of the joint, glowing faintly.

—In 1904, Russia and Japan were at war over trade routes, resources, and influence in Manchuria.

—OK, Nolan says, settling in.

—Czar Nicholas II ordered his entire Baltic Fleet to the Sea of Japan after the defeat of his Pacific Fleet at the hands of the Japanese navy. That's halfway around the world, mind you.

Using the end of the joint, Cosmo punctuates his points in the space before them.

—It took the Baltic Fleet eight months to travel 18,000 nautical miles, and when they arrived in the Strait of Tsushima, they were weary. Morale was low. Their ships were slowed considerably by a year's accumulation of barnacles. Long story short, the Japanese annihilate the czar's entire Baltic Fleet in less than two days.

Cosmo holds up two fingers.

—Two.

He runs his free hand through his hair.

—The war between Russia and Japan ends several months later. Japan is established as a modern world power and, according to many historians, the Russian defeat was a primary cause of the Russian Revolution, brainchild of that wonderful slogan, "Don't be a slave to material things," which, it turns out, is the perfect banner for a consumerist society. It encourages disposability.

—You throw bleach on the neighbors' lawn, Chance?

—No.

—You swear.

—I didn't throw it.

Then, under his breath:

—I *wrote* with it. In order to leave them a message.

—You can't do shit like that, Chance.

—Don't foist your morals on me.

—My morals? You're the one writing a manifesto.

—This transcends the manifesto.

—Knock on their door.

—Nah.

—Scared?

—Of what?

Cosmo looks at Nolan.

—Confrontation.

—Have you ever known me to shy from confrontation?

—Then knock on the door.

—Have you not been listening? They do not process information in that way, Nolan. Now is the time to fight fire with fire.

Nolan looks down at his beer.

—You ain't the one starting those fires, are you, Chance?

—No, but I'm flattered you'd ask.

—Chance?

—No, Nolan. But even if I was, I wouldn't tell you.

—Why not?

—Because that's a felony offense, and if I'm going to commit a well-planned felony, I wouldn't utter word one about it to anyone but the voices in my own head.

—Thanks for putting me at ease.

—That's not the reason I'm on this planet.

—What are you on this planet for?

Cosmo offers Nolan the joint, but Nolan raises his hand.

—Lightweight, Cosmo says.

—Everything in moderation.

—Except beer.

—Except beer.

Then, Nolan asks:

—So how's this Russian story of yours connected to the movie?

—It's not.

—I thought everything's connected.

—Well, yes, in that sense, I guess it is.

—How, then?

—I'd have to consider the ways some before responding.

—Stumped the boy genius.

—Don't call me that. I hated when he called me that.

Nolan takes a sip of his beer and then lowers it into his lap. Fingering the label, he asks:

—Dawn know you tried joining the Marines?

Cosmo tips his head back and blows a geyser of smoke at the sky. Bringing his head back down, he nods.

—Yep.

—And?

—When we invaded Iraq, she said, "Just think, that could've been you."

Nolan scratches at his cheek and says:

—You wished it was you, though, didn't you?

—Part of me. At the time. Yeah, I did.

—I thought about it, too, when we went into Afghanistan. Not about Iraq, but I did for Afghanistan.

—The Good War.

—Yeah.

—You would've made a good soldier. You're a good shot.

—Better than you.

—We both know that's not true, Nolan.

—Remember the time Dad took us out to that salt flat, out in Nevada?

—I do.

—He brought that smallboy of helium so we could sit around shooting red balloons all day.

—I remember you missing.

—"Who knew the boy genius would be such a good shot?"

—He only called me that because I was better with words than you all were. Better shot, too.

—Yes, you were.

—A better shot?

—With words. Than me or him.

—Better builder, too.

—Where's that coming from?

—Remember the cow-man I built?

—No.

—You don't?

—No.

—I took all those cow bones we found on the flat and arranged them to resemble a dead man with a cow's head and huge schlong.

—Of course you did.

—There's a picture of that somewhere. I think I'm lying down next to him.

—Strange bedfellows.

The brothers sit quietly for a second or two before Cosmo says:

—You ever look at those boys coming back and wish it were you, knowing what we know now, how most of it went over there?

—No.

—I wish I could have seen it, though.

—That sounds mighty naïve coming from someone smart as you.

—You wouldn't even want to see it? Just a glimpse?

—Why would you want to see that?

—Because that's how all this works. Everything around us. You think all this plastic just materialized out of thin air? Motherfucker, we suck this shit out of the earth.

—Language, Nolan mutters.

—I mean, you wake up, you make coffee, you shower, skip breakfast, go to work, eat a sandwich, the bread's soggy, you go home, you drink a beer and play video games, order take out, drink three more beers, and you fall asleep.

—You do.

—Yes, that's my routine, my habit, so you can see why I might be interested in a change of scenery, in a chance to see what all runs the machine.

—That'd be a change of scenery all right.

—For a while there, I didn't care if it was a just war or not, I just wanted to see it. I mean every fucking Sunday a bunch of slobbering drunks dress up like drag queens for football games, hands on their glittery puffed out chests, everybody up for the anthem, a song I love, by the way, while boys in Najaf are engaged in hand-to-hand combat in a cemetery. Did you know Muqtada al-Sadr's got, like, two, three years on you? Imagine all he's done, what he's seen.

—I'd like to see him cut a roof.

—He's better at bringing them down.

—That's my point.

Then:

—Are you in contact with Dawn?

—No.

—None?

—I forward all of her mail to her parents. No one calls here for her anymore.

—What went wrong?

—I don't want to talk about that, Nolan.

—You'll talk about war but not your ex-wife?

—Not all stories need to be told.

Cosmo belches.

—You still planting daffodils at Dad's grave?

—I am.

—Mom likes that.

—She does.

Then:

—When Dad gave you his lighter, did he say anything to you?

—What do you mean?

—When he gave me my .38, he said don't be an idiot.

—He didn't say that.

—Not exactly, but he said don't hurt anyone who doesn't have it coming.

—OK.

—He say anything to you when he gave you that lighter?

—Yeah, he did.

—What'd he say?

—Don't be an idiot.

Nolan smiles.

—Not going to tell me, are you?

—He didn't say it to you, did he?

—No.

—That's because he said it to me. That's mine, not yours.

—I'm glad you weren't there, Cosmo. In Afghanistan or Iraq.
Cosmo doesn't respond.

—I remember sitting in a bar in San Francisco, listening to all the arguments for and against—

—People in San Francisco against the war? Shocking.

—There's good people in San Francisco, Cos—

—They should spend more of their weekends there. Buy their second homes there, too.

—Like them buying here isn't driving your property value up.

—We'll see how long it's my property.

Nolan doesn't respond. He hears the voices in the backyard down the way, but he can't discern any meaning from them. He checks the level in his beer, lets his eyes linger there for a moment before saying:

—I can remember thinking about how much you wanted to be there, in that TV, part of something historic, like Dad was.

Cosmo shakes his head.

—You need to remind me not to share my good stuff with you anymore.

—Because you think keeping advertisements out of movies is going to make the world a better place?

—Because I think it's a start.

A scream comes from the house down the way. A scream followed by swearing. Nolan looks to Cosmo.

—You dumped that entire bottle out, didn't you? Nolan asks.

—This is my battle, Cosmo says. This is where my war is waged.

Nolan looks away from his brother as Cosmo says:

—The thing is, though, I'm losing.

8

Iridescent strands of fiberglass insulation sift down on Manny and Nolan as they pull the last of the sheetrock from a second-story bedroom ceiling. Tiny black mouse droppings rain down the fronts of their work shirts. They take turns packing the insulation into the contractor-grade sacks and hauling the sacks into the master bedroom, where the empty window spaces overlook the trash pile in the driveway below. Nolan stares down into the jumbled mass of black bags, sheetrock, wallpaper, and old wood and glass they've amassed. Downstairs, Guillermo is pounding new fir sticks into walls that may very well lie heaped in some future pile, destined for some future landfill, for some future ocean.

When Nolan re-enters the bedroom, he finds Manny standing on the ladder, crowbar in hand, quietly inspecting the bottom cord of a truss.

—*¿Qué pasa?* Nolan asks.

—No good.

—*Por qué* no good?

—*Termitas.*

—Termites?

—*Sí, termitas. Mira.*

Manny jumps down, and Nolan climbs the ladder and begins tracing the tunnels with the claw of his hammer, as if using it to decipher some hieroglyphs there.

—No good. Nolan shakes his head.

—Ching-ching. Manny smiles, rubbing his index finger along the underside of his thumb. Ching-ching for Joe.

—*Sí*, Nolan says. Ching-ching. We better tell your brother.

Manny calls to Guillermo, who lumbers up the stairs and into the room with a carpenter's pencil in one hand and a carpenter's square and tape measure in the other. He is the only accomplished carpenter Nolan has ever met who doesn't wear pouches. At first he discounted this in Guillermo, but during his time on the farmhouse remodel, he's come to see how it works for the Mexican, who stays light and fast and doesn't waste movements and is always thinking several steps ahead. Once, when Manny and Nolan were carrying a stack of redwood boards from the house to the salvage stack, Manny stopped and moved Guillermo's hammer across the room and on their way back through Guillermo said something to him in Spanish that Nolan didn't understand but that made the younger brother lower his head sheepishly.

Nolan wonders how it must be for the brothers so far from home, from the comforts of a native language, and here not completely by choice, but by necessity. Nolan has little idea what they endure.

At the landfill one morning during his first or second week, he and Manny were unloading the back of Joe's Ram, taking turns launching pieces of wood and sailing flats of sheetrock. Heaps of appliances and recyclable metals were stacked off to the side. They had the place to themselves except for two yellow dozers crushing trash and the gulls flying through dust stirred by the tractors. Nolan and Manny both wore masks.

—Your brother married? Nolan asked.

—No, Manny answered.

—He want to be?

—*No lo sé.*

—You never asked him?

—Maybe I ask him he no want a wife, and he think I ask, you *joto*?

—Is he?

—No. He is *tímido.* You know this word? *Tímido?*

—I wouldn't call Guillermo timid.

—What is it?

—Timid.

—Timid.

—Yeah. But what he is, is shy.

—Shy.

—Shy. Timid is different.

—In Spanish is *tímido.*

—Funny how that works.

—*¿Cómo?*

—Nothing.

A few seconds later, Nolan said:

—He's a good carpenter.

—Yes, but is not only thing.

—You try telling him that?

Manny smiled behind his mask.

—You tell.

—He really lift a burro off the ground?

—*Sí.* Two times.

—Yeah, I'll stay out of it.

At that point, a flatbed with plywood sides rolled up and

parked right next to them. Three Mexicans jumped out of the bench seat and walked around to the back of the truck and while one opened the doors to the sides, the other two climbed over and began unloading their own load of sheetrock and two-by-fours. Nolan looked over now and then, impressed by how quickly they worked. They had the truck empty just as he and Manny were emptying the Ram. Not one of the Mexicans wore gloves or protective eyewear or a mask. At the end of the workday, Nolan would stand at the back spigot at the farmhouse and wash sheetrock and wood dust off his face and neck and when he got home his eyes were bloodshot from the fiberglass insulation. Despite wearing masks, his hankies would be streaked with black snot. When he turned to mention to Manny that the Mexicans weren't wearing masks, he noticed that Manny had removed his and it was tucked in his back pocket. Nolan didn't say anything at all, not even after they were gone and Manny put his mask on again.

Back in the upstairs bedroom, Guillermo climbs the ladder and after a moment he climbs down and moves it down the way and climbs it again to inspect a second and third cord. When he comes down from the ladder he places his tools on the treads and takes his cell phone from his back pocket and after pushing several buttons with his thumb he holds the phone out to Nolan.

—What? Nolan says.

—You tell, Manny says for his brother.

Nolan looks at Guillermo, and the Mexican nods down at his phone.

—You, is all he says.

—All right, Nolan says, turning to Manny, but you tell your brother he owes me a six-pack for this.

★

He dreams one night he's standing on the bank of the river watching the farmhouse burn on the other side. The light from the flames plays on the dark surface of the water, slender tongues lapping at the reflection of the full moon. At first he's alone, listening to the crackles and hisses of the fire, of walls and floors collapsing inside, sending sparks through the windows that turn into stars in the night sky. But then he's with Cosmo. They're boys, standing across the river from the house fire. Nolan grabs his brother by the arm, pulls on him to leave, but Cosmo doesn't budge.

—No, he says to Nolan. Don't.

Joe shows up late for work on Monday with his hammer arm in a dishtowel sling and a rattlesnake's rattle sealed in a clear plastic sandwich bag, beaded white on the inside from the humidity of its decomposition.

—I walk out to the truck for my checkbook last night. It's late. I'm barefoot. I have Joey in my arms, and I haven't eaten yet.

Manny holds up the plastic bag, looking at the rattle, rotating it from side to side, the rattle writing in cursive on the inside of the bag through the tiny beads of moisture gathered there.

—I hear this *tst-tst-tst-tst* in the dark, and the first thing I think is, Shit, bro, not tonight. Please don't be a leak in the gas line, not tonight.

Joe's voice, his tone and cadence, sounds practiced with the telling of the story inside his own head on the ride over.

—So I get the checkbook, and I'm standing there, with my face shoved out in the dark, just sniffing for it, you know, looking behind my wife's flower pots, not realizing that Joey's picking his nose at eye level with the damn thing until, I think, Dude, the hookup's on the other side of the house.

—You need glasses? Nolan asks.

—I'm going to spring for the laser work someday.

Manny pinches the rattle stub, takes it from the baggy, shakes it and whistles.

—*Muy viejo.*

—Fuck, yes, it's old, Joe says.

Then Guillermo says something to Manny in Spanish that Nolan doesn't understand but that Manny relates to Joe and Nolan both:

—In Mexico, our father, he have two, three this big.

—Bullshit, Joe says to Guillermo. *Este, este es el hombre.*

Guillermo shrugs and walks off. Joe continues:

—My wife's inside whipping up tofu stir-fry with the TV on. Her daughter's on the telephone. Again. I set Joey down inside the door, turn on the light switch and, boom, there he is, bro, all coiled up and sticking his tongue out at me. Nearly crapped my britches.

—This where you tell us how you messed up your arm? Nolan says.

A smile, wry and satisfied, takes over Joe's suntanned face.

—Well, after the shovel came out, I started swinging like crazy.

—At least you got the snake.

—Yeah, but the wife's flower pots weren't so forgiving.

Nolan comes through the front door after work that evening to the sound of music playing from behind Cosmo's bedroom door. Articles of men's and women's clothing are scattered along the hallway floor. Pant legs pooled and long sleeves flat on the floor, as if reaching out for the ones who left them there. Nolan walks directly into the kitchen, grabs an apple, and is turning to leave when a loud thud sounds from down the hall, followed by a woman's laughter. A few moments later, Cosmo's bedroom door opens, and he walks down the hallway and into the kitchen, naked beneath his robe, his hand pressed against the back of his head, his eyeglasses crooked.

—Some things just can't be done, he says to Nolan while digging in the freezer for an ice pack. I don't care how limber you are.

—Gravity prevail?

—Infinitely.

Cosmo presses the ice pack to the back of his head and leans against the refrigerator door while Nolan rinses the apple in the sink and then wipes it dry on the inside of his shirt.

—I'm going out for a bit.

—Probably best for all parties involved.

Nolan rides to the plaza and chains the bicycle to a newspaper stand in front of The Bull and The Bear. At the Farmers' and Mechanics' Bank across the square, a group of carpenters work on scaffolding under flood lamps. From what Nolan can tell, they're doing a light remodel of the façade to antique it for the film that is due to begin shooting in Burnridge in a week's time. Several clusters of townspeople and tourists stand watching the carpenters' shadows, thrown long against the brightly lit building. Nolan listens to the nail guns thwap and to the circular saws groan and whine.

The marine layer has come in overhead, and the light from the flood lamps brightens the usual red-orange hue of the night to a milky blue. The entire plaza seems altered, somehow, in anticipation of the filming, more presented than usual. It reminds Nolan of a theme park he visited in southern California with a woman he was dating when he was twenty-one. They ate psilocybin mushrooms and walked hand-in-hand beneath the flashing lights and cartoonish images, the people dressed in costumes, the people play-acting characters. Nolan and the woman walked by a group of toughs who made fun of his boots and hat, but he and the woman both looked beyond them, eyes wide and humming, and passed on without further incident.

—Headache, yells one of the carpenters working on the façade as a board falls clattering to the ground from the third-story scaffolding.

Nolan wakes from the memory of the theme park to see his shadow cast before him, lean and tall and jean-jacketed and wearing his white Western hat. We maintain narratives, however false, to survive. Cosmo does. You do. Grant him his lies as he grants you yours.

When Nolan pushes through the swinging doors of The Bull and The Bear, he finds Dave, the bartender, alone in the place, watching a baseball game on television. Nolan sits at the bar, looks it up and down, and then lifts his hands to Dave as if to say, where is everyone? To which Dave replies:

—They heard you were on your way over.

—Slip me a few bucks and I'll drink elsewhere.

—Nah, then those assholes would be here.

Then, setting a napkin in front of Nolan:

—What'll it be?

—Top-shelf whiskey and a half draft back, please.

The bartender sets the shot glass on the bar and fills it. Then, he walks down to the draft handles. At the back of the barroom, near the bathroom doors, the green felt of the pool table glows under a stained-glass chandelier. A chalkboard, screwed to the wall beyond, bears names from previous competitions. Lou, Al, FC, Tom, Android. The jukebox stands unplugged in the corner beneath a set of plaques for Meatloaf, Spaghetti, and Chili contests. Dave sets the beer in front of Nolan.

—Where's numb nuts?

—He made a new friend.

—Yeah, I met her. Two trains, wrecking in the night.

Nolan shakes his head and smiles, his eyes on the whiskey as he sips.

—You really his brother? Dave asks, wiping down the bar with a damp rag.

—I am.

—And you admit to that?

—You seem like the compassionate sort.

—Ha, Dave laughs. Good one.

—Looks like they're cleaning up the old bank across the way, Nolan says, setting the glass down on the bar.

—Hard to miss with all the lights. They'll probably spend more time working on it than they do actually using the damn thing.

—No doubt, Nolan says, watching the streaks momentarily catch the bar's light before fading away completely.

—From what I hear, Dave says, it's going to be more of a car commercial than anything else.

—I heard that, too.

—Apparently it's based on a true story, but they're changing the ending so that the lady drives off into the sunset.

—Probably wouldn't make a very good commercial if the car drives off a cliff.

—No, it wouldn't. Dave smiles.

Nolan looks into the empty shot glass before him.

—Hollywood stretches the truth, he says.

—Hell, we all do, they just make money at it.

—*En México*, Manny says the next morning as he and Nolan are on the roof removing an old aluminum antenna and accompanying guy wires, I meet this man. He has many cow. They eat the grass. But two places, *hay un cercado.* How you say?

—Fence.

—*Sí*, two places *hay mucho* grass in the fence. *Está muy alto.* *¿Entiendes?*

—*Sí*, the grass is tall in the fenced area but *no en los otros lugares*.

—I say to this man, "Why you no have you cows there?" He say, "Is special places. Is where I have my first time." *¿Entiendes? No más un virgen.*

—All right. Nolan smiles.

—Then, I say, "*Y el otro* place. *¿Qué pasó allá?* What happen there?" He say, "Her parents watch there." I say, "Her parents? They watch?" "*Sí*," he say. I say, "What they say when they see you?"

Nolan looks over at the Mexican, grinning that grin of his.

—He say, "They say, 'Moo.'"

Nolan calls Linda on his ride home from work that day from the phone booth in front of the Chinese restaurant.

—Hello.

—Hear me out.

—What do you want, Nolan?

—Just hear me out.

—Fine. What?

—I was walking by this pasture the other day and there's this guy there, with all his cows.

—Are you really doing this?

—Except, he's got these two spots in the pasture that are fenced off where the grass grows tall. So, I ask him, "Why're those two spots fenced off?" And he says, "Well, that one there's where I lost my virginity." "And the other one?" I ask. "That's where her parents stood and watched." "They what?" I said. "Yeah," he says. "They stood and watched." "What'd they say when they saw you?" I ask him. And he says: "Moo."

A second or two later, Linda states:

—That's funny.

—How are you?

—I'm fine. Really good actually.

—Yeah?

—Yeah, I'm getting ready for a date.

Nolan doesn't respond, and Linda pounces on his silence with:

—And how are you?

—I'm all right.

—Where are you?

—Northern California.

—What's up there?

—My brother. He writes for a newspaper up here.

—And here I didn't even know you had a brother.

Nolan can hear the radio on in the background, the voices conversing.

—He's a couple years older than me.

—Are you staying with him?

—Yeah, in his garage.

—Lovely. Are you working?

—I am.

—Tracts?

—No, a remodel actually.

Linda doesn't respond. He can feel her letting him fill the silence.

—I'm mostly doing the grunt work on this one. It's been pretty neat, you know, exposing the work of others, their cuts, the joints and seams and stuff. I like seeing that.

—Is it old?

—At least eighty years.

—Wow.

—Not a straight line in the place.

—Let's see you in eighty years.

—Right. Nolan smiles.

He bites the inside of his lip. He's got her listening and he knows that if he allows her a word in edgewise he'll lose her, so he does what comes least naturally: he talks.

—Did you know old window glass gets thicker along the bottom sill than along the top? It settles with time.

—Can't say that I did.

—I knew an apprentice carpenter down in LA; he said he found five grand hidden in a wall once. It was wrapped in a newspaper dated December 8, 1941.

—Lot of money back then.

—Lot of money today.

—Sure it is.

—Another guy I know found a stash of women's underwear tucked away in a wall.

—Did he keep them?

—I don't know.

—Did he?

—Yes.

—Men are disgusting.

—I once came across a bunch of business cards with dates inked on the back. One of them had a friendly "Up Yours" written on it.

—Just another way of marking your territory.

—That's not it.

—What is it, then?

—A hundred years ago, everyone probably knew the people who built their homes.

—Do you really think that's true?

—Not in every situation, no, but in most, I bet you did. Hell, I know it was a lot more than today.

—OK, so?

—Sometimes, I think about all the places I've been, all the walls I've raised, no one knows it was me except the guys I worked alongside, and even they—

—What, you want your name in lights?

—I didn't say that.

—What are you saying, then?

—I guess leaving behind cards or signing a wall or a joist is just our way of communicating with each other. Of saying, look, I was here, too. It's not always a signature. I've come across vulgar pictures, hand drawn and photographed.

—You keep any of them?

—No.

—Did you?

—No, but once, on a lath board in the closet of this one house, I found a pencil drawing of a swan, dated 1905. I kept that. Just some old timer's way of signing his work, of saying, I was here, like putting your name in concrete.

Nolan feels like he's said all that he has to say, but there's more, and he doesn't know how to say it all, so he doesn't, and in the silence that ensues he feels like he's losing her until she speaks, and not to challenge him, not to snap at him, not to condescend in warranted hurt and understandable anger:

—In the museum at school, there's a collection of old Indian baskets.

She hesitates.

—I mean Native American.

—I know what you mean, he says.

—This one woman, her baskets are highly regarded. Apparently, she would put a mis-weave in every one she made. She never put it the same place, and never where you'd immediately notice it, but when you did, the basket never looked the same again, and you knew straightaway that it was one of hers.

—I like that, Nolan says, the receiver warm against his head.

—Me, too.

—How is school?

—School's school.

Nolan tests the waters:

—Don't tell me, then.

—Don't pretend you're interested, she responds, not harshly, but in the way she would in the past.

—I wouldn't have asked if I wasn't.

—You also wouldn't have left the way you did if you were. He pushed it.

—Fair enough.

—Yeah, she says, fair enough.

—So how's school? he tries again.

—I don't know. She sighs.

—Why's that?

—I'm having second thoughts about the prospect of looking into people's mouths and smelling their breaths for the next twenty-five years.

—Don't you all wear those little blue masks?

—Very funny.

—So, what then?

—I don't know. I really like my teachers, and for the most part I get along with all the other girls, but I don't know. I think I might want to study something else.

—Like what?

—I don't know. For the first time in my life, I really give a shit about school, and I'm good at it, and now I worry I've settled for dental hygiene because it's safe.

—Nothing wrong with that.

—No, but, I guess I just never saw myself in college, and now that I'm here, even though I'm the oldest one in the class, I don't see myself anywhere else.

—Yeah, Nolan says.

Linda gets quiet. He doesn't want to press her further, but he doesn't want to get off the phone with her either, so he says:

—It's a good group of guys I'm working with. This kid, Manny, and his older brother, Guillermo. You'd get a kick out of Manny. Kid never shuts up. He's the one who told me that joke.

—It's a good one.

—Yeah.

—So, your brother's a writer?

—A reporter, yeah.

—That's got to be exciting.

—There's a firebug running around town here, setting old houses on fire.

—I haven't heard that word in I don't know how long. Since my grandpa was alive, probably.

—What's that, firebug?

—Yeah.

—That's not what he's calling him in the paper.

—I hope not.

—Yeah.

—What's it like there?

—It's wine country.

—Nice.

—Yeah. Chance moved here with his wife a few years back when he got the job at the paper. She was a yoga instructor. They bought a house for way too much and now he's in it on his own.

—Why'd she leave?

—I don't know.

—Did you ask him?

—We don't talk about that kind of stuff.

—You mean important stuff?

—I asked, and he didn't say.

—What's her name?

—Dawn. She left him for the real-estate agent that sold them the house.

—Ouch.

—Yep.

—How's he doing with that?

Nolan thinks a few seconds before answering.

—He's brittle. He means well, but he's got his head wrapped tight around everything and it's making him paranoid. That, and all the pot he smokes.

—That'll do it.

—Yes, it will.

—Maybe he's the firebug?

—No, I asked him.

—Really?

—Yes.

—I was joking. What'd he say?

—He said he was flattered.

—That's weird. Why?

—It's a long story.

—Yeah.

Nolan knows what's coming, but he's OK with it; he's re-established a line of communication. He knows he can call again, and soon.

—Listen, Linda says, allowing her words to taper off.

—Yeah, I know. I just wanted to share that joke with you.

—Thanks for that.

—I'll talk to you later.

—OK.

—Bye, Linda.

—Bye.

At the end of June, they celebrate Guillermo's thirty-third birthday by going for tacos after work at a taqueria at the south end of town.

—My treat, hombres, Joe says as they stand in an awkward group at the counter.

—¿Sí? You treat? Manny smiles, looking up at the menu

and pulling at his chin with his thumb and forefinger in mock contemplation.

—Why don't you go play something on the jukebox? Joe says.

—¿*Cómo*?

—*Cómo*, my ass, amigo. You heard me.

They sit at a heavily painted picnic table on the outdoor patio in the shade of an umbrella clad in beer advertisements. It was a hot workday, and Joe and Nolan drink Mexican beer with limes while Manny has an orange soda and Guillermo a glass bottle of cola. A napkin dispenser and hot-sauce bottle stand near the pole to the umbrella and salt specks are scattered on the table.

At the far end of the patio, a trio of concrete workers sit with two empty six-packs of beer on the table before them. One table over from this, a handsome young woman sits across from a tall, light-skinned, dark-haired man wearing a two-piece suit. The woman is short and dark skinned and voluptuous. She wears a red scarf about her neck and speaks in a heavily accented English, to which the man she's with responds without an accent, but something about his pronunciation makes Nolan suspects that English is not his first language either.

Nolan looks to the couple because that is where Guillermo is looking. Meanwhile, Manny raises his chin toward the overpass where southbound traffic is stop and go.

—Maybe *hay un accidente*? Manny says.

—Maybe, Joe responds.

—Is maybe *un Ram*.

—You little wise-ass. Joe smiles. Here I buy you dinner and you start in on this.

A waitress emerges from inside the restaurant carrying a red plastic tray laden with two plastic baskets of fried corn tortilla chips and four *salsitas*, two *pico de gallo*, two *chili verde*. While Manny and Joe argue over American-made automobiles, Nolan watches Guillermo pick at the tortilla chips and glance over now and then at the young woman.

—No, no, no. Joe waves his finger at Manny. You don't know, man. You just *no comprendes*.

The tall, dark-haired man sitting with the young woman stands, steps over the bench seat, smooths down the front of his jacket and heads toward the bathroom. Once he's gone, the woman removes her scarf and sets it on her purse on the bench seat at her side.

In the six weeks that Nolan has been on the remodel, he and Guillermo have exchanged only a few words, and even then only one or two that weren't about the work at hand.

—Manny, Joe says, for your job. OK? For your *trabajo*, it is *muy importante* that you *comprendes* that *un Camaro es mejor que un Mustang*. OK? Bitchin Camaro, Manny. Bitchin. Camaro.

—*No mames güey*. Manny shakes his head, his face scrunched.

Nolan watches the young woman spoon salsa on a chip instead of dipping it. There's something about the way she dabs a napkin at the corner of her mouth and sits looking with her head turned to traffic on the street that makes Nolan think she's aware of Guillermo watching her.

One of the concrete workers stands and walks unsteadily down the aisle. As he brushes past the woman, her scarf lifts from the top of her purse and Guillermo slides off the end of his seat, takes two steps, and snatches the scarf just before it touches the ground. He straightens his back and offers it to the woman.

—Thank you, she says in English.

—You welcome, Guillermo mumbles.

The man the woman is dining with returns just as Guillermo is making his way back to his seat. As they pass one another, Guillermo nods to the man, who responds by lifting his chin at the carpenter.

The man and the woman leave soon after this and when they're gone Nolan says to Manny in English that a raised chin is no way to acknowledge a man's nod and he agrees and speaks in kind to his brother in Spanish but Guillermo doesn't respond.

—I'd like to see that ponce even try, Joe says, swallowing the last swig of his beer. Burros, eh, Billy?

Guillermo shakes his head.

—He-haw, Joe groans loudly. He-haw.

When Guillermo doesn't smile, Joe stands and mimes struggling to lift a heavy animal.

—He-haw, he yells. He-haw.

The gesture is obscene and the concrete workers at the other table begin pointing and laughing at him, and Manny is laughing and Nolan is smiling and chuckling, and then, finally, Guillermo begins to smile, as well.

9

Monday morning Nolan rides up the gravel road to the farmhouse to find Joe pacing in front of the trash heap. The fog has burned off early and the heat of the day has already chased off shadows cast by the surrounding oaks. Joe's serape is draped over the driver's-side window of the Ram and he's sweating through the underarms of a light-brown T-shirt with the words *Hecho en México* written in bold black letters across his chest. His arm is suspended in the dishtowel sling, his free hand holding a cell phone to the side of his head. Manny and Guillermo, Nolan notices, always the first ones on the job, have yet to arrive.

—Listen, Joe says into the phone, my guy's here. I have to go.

Nolan leans the woman's bicycle against the oak and undoes his lunch sack from the handlebars. Scarves of lace lichen dangle listlessly from the oak, their shadows playing over Nolan's hands as he unties the knot.

—Yeah, Joe says into the phone. No, I will. Thanks.

Joe collapses the phone against his hip and slides it into the back pocket of his faded work jeans.

—Morning, Nolan says.

—Guillermo and Manny got deported.

—What?

—Manny got arrested over the weekend for drunk driving.

—But Manny doesn't drink.

—And he wasn't driving, either.

—I'm confused, Nolan says.

—Apparently, Manny and his wife got in an argument. Afterwards, he took a sniff of a beer and climbed in the front seat of Guillermo's truck and started revving the engine outside their apartment. When the cops showed, Manny resisted, and that's when Guillermo got involved.

—So they hauled him off, too.

—And neither of them have cards.

—There's nothing we can do?

—My lawyer friend says no. He said Manny's been stopped twice coming over, and if he tries a third time, they'll lock him up. Guillermo won't be able to make it back for at least a month, if at all.

—What about Manny's family?

—Their other brother is going to take them down.

Joe kicks the tire of his Ram, and his long, sandy-blond hair converges over his face and eyes. Tucking it back behind his ears, he says:

—Shit.

Nolan looks to the gravel road, then out over the valley. The vineyards are dark green with jungly vines, the hills tawny below the dark chaparral of Fumarole Peak. Heat radiates above the valley floor.

—Listen, man, Joe says, I know I haven't used you right, and I'll give you a raise, or whatever, I just can't afford to fall behind on this place, especially with the termites.

—I'm not going anywhere.

—You mean that?

—I do.

—Thanks, man.

They stand for a few seconds until Nolan says:

—You all right?

—I mean, Manny and I, we had our moments, for sure, but I don't wish any wrong his way.

—I know it.

—And Guillermo? Little bull's like a younger brother.

Joe sighs. He places the tip of his tongue in an upper molar and shakes his head with his lip snarled a bit, not in anger, but to hold back his emotions. Then, he says:

—My wife's sister's kid's going to help out until I can find someone more substantial, but, we're good here for now?

—No worries, Nolan says.

—No worries, huh? Joe smiles, finally looking Nolan in the eyes.

—It's all good. Nolan grins.

The next morning, Joe arrives at the farmhouse with a sixteen-year-old kid slouched in the passenger seat of his Ram. Straight off, Nolan doesn't like the look of him. Joe says a few words to the kid, who smiles and says something back, to which Joe just shakes his head as he slides out of the truck.

Nolan walks out to meet the contractor.

—Shouldn't he be in school? Nolan asks.

—School's out for the summer. Besides, they already gave him the boot.

—I'm not a babysitter, Joe.

—He's a temporary fix.

Over Joe's shoulder, Nolan watches the kid lift a new tool belt from the bed of Joe's truck. It has clean cloth bags and a hammer nestled in the holster. Sunlight glints off the shiny head of the 21-oz black-handled framer. Nolan squints to make out what the kid has written along the handle in yellow grease marker.

—Does he even know how to swing that thing?

—He wants to be a carpenter, bro. He wants to learn the trade. That still means something, right?

Nolan looks over at the kid. He wears cowboy boots, faded black denims, a black-and-white thin-striped two-button work shirt, and a mesh baseball cap, the greasy brim folded into a tight, inverted V. He has patchy facial hair and a fat dip of chewing tobacco tucked behind his lower lip. He's buckled the tool belt and slung it over his shoulder and he stands leaning back against the truck bed with his boot heel jacked up on the tire behind him. He casually twirls the hammer around his index finger like a gunslinger.

Joe says:

—Mason, come here.

And over swaggers the kid.

—Mason, Joe says, this is Nolan Jackson. Nolan, Mason Drove.

The kid flips the hammer into his left palm and offers Nolan his right.

—Friends call me Mace.

Nolan extends his hand and they shake. He meets the kid's eyes, and they do not waver.

—So, Mace says, stepping back and looking over the farmhouse, what the hell happened here?

Nolan looks down at the kid's hammer, holstered in its

steel loop, and sees the word DEATHSTICK smeared in one long yellow word, the letters like broken teeth in a rotten smile.

Throughout the workday, Mace spits fat globs of tobacco juice in a plastic soda bottle he keeps in his nail bags. At lunch he devours a white-bread and processed-ham sandwich, a snack bag of corn chips, and two cans of cola. Then, he sits back and lights an unfiltered cigarette.

Bullets, he calls them.

He smokes each bullet down to a finger-pinched nub that he stubs out on the heel of his black cowboy boot before bringing his hand level with his head and flicking the butt with his middle finger out to the trash heap. The carelessness of the action is a not so subtle reminder of how much Nolan misses working with Los Hermanos de Zacatecas.

For three days Nolan and the kid work side by side without speaking to one another about anything besides the framing of walls, the hauling of trash, or the salvaging of hardware and wood. But on the fourth day, as they sit on the front porch of the farmhouse for lunch while Joe's gone to the lumber yard for materials, it's Mace who finally breaks the silence:

—Bummer about Joe's Mexicans getting deported.

—Yes, it is.

—Of course, I guess we wouldn't be sitting here like this if they hadn't.

Nolan doesn't respond, which leaves space for the kid to say:

—All pans out in the wash, right?

Nolan clenches his jaw and looks out over the vineyards. He can hear cicada in the oak canopy above. A scrub jay's squawk.

—How long since you been a journeyman, Jackson?

—I was a little older than you when I got started.

—How old are you now?

—Almost thirty-two.

—Shit, you look older than that.

Mace leans back against the two-by-ten Guillermo cut for his noon-time rest. He cups his hands behind his head and crosses his ankles. Nolan notices scars on the heels of the kid's boots where he stubs out his bullets.

—You like being a journeyman? he asks Nolan.

—I do.

—I don't want to be nothing else. Not never. I just love pounding nails. I bet it gets to be hard on the body, though, at your age.

Nolan nods, but barely.

—Where're you from? Mason asks.

—Here and there.

—You married?

—Nope.

—Ever been?

—Nope.

—You like working for Joe?

—I do.

—No, I mean, do you like having a boss at your age? I know I wouldn't.

At the end of the first week with Mace on the job, Nolan rides into the hills west of town to clear his mind. The kid shows up on time, he works steadily at what he's told to do, he asks questions when he doesn't understand, he asks questions when he does. He's a solid apprentice who is genuinely interested in carpentry and construction and he enjoys the labor. Nolan can see this in the way the kid handles the tools, in the way he's getting a feel for them, experimenting with the weight of a circular saw, extending a tape across a room. He doesn't swing or cut blindly. Ultimately, he reminds Nolan of himself. And yet Nolan has been making speeches in his head throughout the week to Joe about why he's quitting and to Cosmo about why he's going to leave Burnridge. In the past, Nolan has simply hitched up and moved on at first inklings like these. But this time he can't leave, not yet. If he leaves now, Linda will see it as weakness and she'll be right. And he'll be leaving Cosmo, who needs him at the house, if only to cook and to clean and to listen.

So Nolan rides. He rides to exhaust his body in hopes that his mind will follow and he'll be able to sleep without drinking himself closer to exhaustion. He rides to work out the frustration that has accrued from working all week with the kid, who has a recklessness about him, an arrogance outside of the work that Nolan distrusts.

In the woods, miles from town, he rides up on a set of fluorescent orange traffic cones and a sheriff's patrol car blocking the road. A young mustachioed deputy sits in the driver's seat with the door open. He has a cell phone open before him, and his thumbs tap at the keys. He smiles to himself, his moustache almost twitching.

Nolan stops before the patrol car and unscrews the cap from his water bottle. Fifty yards beyond the deputy and his vehicle, several men and one woman stand around a camera set on a tripod near where a gravel road turns off the asphalt back road and disappears into the woods. The woman holds a portable, two-way radio up to her mouth. One of the men walks to the side of the road, a cell phone to his ear, absentmindedly kicking a rock.

—Nice bike, the deputy says to Nolan without looking up from his cell phone.

—Make me an offer.

—It hot?

—You know a lot of grown men who steal women's bicycles. Pink ones at that?

—You'd be surprised.

Nolan drinks from his water bottle.

—This that movie? he asks.

—More like a car commercial.

The deputy's two-way radio squawks and jargon comes through that Nolan can't make out. The deputy looks to the woman, who waves to him, to which he responds in kind.

—Road's closed, the deputy says in an official tone of voice.

Nolan can hear the sound of automobile engines revving in the woods, deep and throaty in the dusky shadows.

—You might want to stick around for this, the deputy says. Last time through, the car almost rolled.

The engine noise grows louder, more dense as it approaches. The road looks empty and expectant in a way Nolan has never seen a road look before. As the sound swells around them, the deputy's cell phone beeps, tiny and meek, but audible through the engines' roar. He removes the phone from his shirt pocket, flips back the display, presses a button with his thumb, and shakes his head. Smiling to himself, he says:

—Chick's crazy.

As he collapses the phone against his leg, a red convertible speeds along the gravel road with two patrol cars in pursuit. Following closely behind the three vehicles is a flatbed truck with a camera mounted above the cab. A group of people, clad in black, cling to the paneled sides.

The red convertible screeches on the asphalt, its back end swings out, and blue scarves of smoke unravel from its spinning tires. Gravel scatters across the asphalt. The patrol cars follow after, but the flatbed slows to a stop off to the side so that the camera on the tripod can pick up the tail end of the action. Before long, Nolan sees brake lights red in the maple shadows. The three cars stop and pull back around.

—That's about the sixth time they've done that, the deputy says. I asked them about all the track they're laying. All the skid marks. But all they said was, "Oh, we'll clean that up in post-production." I said, "No, I mean, how are you going to get all the skid marks off the road?" "It's all done with computers," they said. Like that's what I meant.

Nolan sits on the love seat untangling a jumbled handful of eight-penny nails. When he arrived home, the check for the remaining balance from his insurance company was waiting for him in the mailbox. He figured out what was in the envelope by the font used to write the return address, that and by the plastic window revealing his name and address. The first non-PO box he's had in years.

The washing machine by the door to the house jerks into its spin cycle and a mop handle vibrates against the side of the hot-water heater. Nolan sorts out one nail at a time, with the tip pointed toward him, ready to be flipped away and hammered. He sets each nail on a new road atlas, splayed open on the cushion and beside the bright white envelope with its crinkly, clear-plastic window with beveled corners.

The garage door is raised on its galvanized tracks, and a

light breeze wends through and out the open side door. With the tip of the last nail, Nolan traces a skinny line south and west from Burnridge, south and west to the ocean, to Point Bonita. He thinks about what the envelope contains, what it stands for, what its contents portend. It's a considerable sum of money, but the slip of paper feels flimsy and insubstantial. He traces the coastline to Año Nuevo, Harmony, Purissima, all the way to San Clemente. He turns to the back of the atlas, to Mexico, and finds Zacatecas. Then, he turns the pages to Nevada, to the city of meadows. He can see her at work, standing at the bar while ordering drinks and unloading her tray of dirties. Sliding back strands of hair behind her ears with the end of a ballpoint pen. The forgotten movements of her workday.

A car drives past the open garage door, its headlights intersecting with the headlights of an oncoming vehicle. On the top of one of Cosmo's cardboard boxes, directly across from Nolan, stands the blue glass canning jar Nolan unearthed when he and Manny were digging the footings. Alongside the jar is a bird's nest Nolan found on one of his bicycle rides after work. His .38 is still buried at the bottom of the cardboard box across from the love seat. He hasn't taken it out in weeks. He hasn't felt the need.

He's made something comfortable of the garage, done so almost instinctively. In front of the love seat, at the foot of his mattress, stands a yard-sale dresser he sanded one Saturday afternoon and stained and later waxed the rails with an unscented candle. His clothes are carefully folded inside each drawer. They are all relatively new. He looks down at the envelope. There's more than enough money promised by that slip of paper for him to buy a new truck, for him to move on.

Unexpectedly, the Valiant's headlights fill the garage with yellow-white light as Cosmo pulls the old vehicle into the driveway. Nolan covers his eyes and stashes the envelope between the love seat's cushions. After Cosmo turns off the engine and the lights, Nolan tucks the atlas beneath his mattress. The door to the Valiant opens and Cosmo climbs out of the car smelling of beer and marijuana smoke. His eyes red slits behind the thick prescription lenses of his eyeglasses.

—He tried burning down the set, Cosmo says, on his way through the garage into the house.

—What set?

—The film set. Down on the plaza. They put it out, of course. Dozens of people standing around, hoping to get in front of the camera, but he went for it, man. Go big, or go home.

Nolan follows Cosmo into the living room, where Cosmo searches the folds of the recliner until, from under the cushion, he lifts his Zippo.

—What a statement, Cosmo says, flipping back the lid on the lighter, striking the flint, and, after it lights, closing it down and putting it in his shirt pocket. You set up this monoculture, the chamber of commerce in concert with local business owners, politicians, farmers, and you smile and invite people from all over the world to come and empty their pockets on your doorsteps. And it works. I have to give it to them; it does. Tourism may just be the most passive-aggressive hustle I can think of.

—Why don't we get some water, sit out back?

But Cosmo isn't listening to Nolan.

—We advertise widely, but that's not enough, so you know what you do?

—I don't know, Nolan says.

—You make this movie. Yes, it's a car commercial, but it's just as much a commercial for Burnridge. I can't believe it took me this long to figure it out. You make up a story, or poach one, as the case may be, filled with idyllic old buildings and scenic back-road chase scenes. I feel evil just uttering it, like I'm giving up the playbook. But someone already figured it out. They sweep into town, refurbish a façade, and boom— lights, camera, action. No need to question monocropping, monoculture, because it's working, right? This place is thriving. Maybe in passing it comes up. Candle-lit dinners. Everyone's feeling a bit tipsy on Chardonnay, noshing arugula and brie when some provocateur, some agitator, some firebug, says, what about the honey bees?

—The honey bees?

—An indicator species. But it's the car's fault, or the oil companies', or some fat-cat caricature of a capitalist in a top hat. To mix metaphors, Nolan, we need a scapegoat. The point is: we *need* someone to blame. We need that effigy because *Who, who, who?* the owl asks. *You, you, you.* And me.

—You need to settle down, Cos.

—But we can't handle that. I can't. I admit it. Someday, the sun will die, and all my beautiful words, sentenced to microfiche, will wither, lost *forever* to a deafening silence, a howling wind that scours the surface of a cold rock that's long since buried our tawdry and feeble remains. But at least he tried, Nolan. At least he played the part of a necessary evil. I think it's important the world know his name.

Cosmo stops pacing. He walks into the kitchen and opens the refrigerator door. When Nolan follows him, he finds the door blocking off much of Cosmo's body, but cold air escapes and bright light shines around him.

—One more thing, Cosmo says, adjusting his glasses.

—What's that?

—I am no longer gainfully employed.

Nolan looks his brother in the eye. The light of the fridge, shining from below, casts upward shadows on his face. Older brother, Nolan thinks. Model and mentor.

—You should see your expression, Cosmo says to Nolan without turning from the fridge.

—What happened?

—Apparently, in journalism, you can't editorialize on the front page.

Cosmo drums his fingers on top of the open door. Over and over, he does this.

—I'm speculating, of course. All the publisher did was hand me an envelope with my last check in it and say, "Your services are no longer needed."

—He's afraid you'll sue.

—She is. And, yes.

Cosmo closes the door and the kitchen is suddenly dim.

—But this gives me time to pursue other endeavors.

—Your book.

—No, that will never be finished.

—What, then?

Leaving the kitchen, Cosmo raises his left index finger to his left eye and, winking, brings it down to point at Nolan as he passes.

—Inquiring minds like mine want to know.

Nolan follows Cosmo into the living room and then into the garage. As Cosmo passes the love seat, he takes the keys to the Valiant from his pocket but stops to survey the garage. He looks over Nolan's stuff, what he's made of the place. Nolan stops in the doorway. Beyond Cosmo, two boys on bikes make intersecting figure eights in the middle of the street, over shadows thrown flat against the asphalt by the street lamps hidden in the trees.

Adjusting his glasses, Cosmo turns to Nolan and, squinting his eyes speculatively, he says:

—You leaving?

—What makes you say that?

—Call it a hunch. A woman's intuition, if you will.

—No.

—But you're thinking about it.

Nolan puts his hands in his pockets and leans against the door jamb.

—Where would I go? he says.

—Does it matter? I thought that was your thing. When the going gets tough, the tough get going.

Cosmo leaves Nolan standing in the doorway. Once the Valiant has pulled away, the street is empty, the subdivision quiet. He hears crickets and the sound of distant traffic. The neighbor's automated watering system switches on. Stepping down into the garage, Nolan notices the mop handle lying on the concrete floor. The washer has finished its cycle and the machine sits at rest again. Nolan bends down to pick it up and in a bucket to the side of the washing machine he notices an empty liter-sized plastic water bottle, a funnel, and a half-empty jug of bleach. Nolan rights the mop and stands looking down into the bucket for a second or two before he picks up the water bottle, unscrews the cap, and brings the mouth slowly to his nose. He sniffs it lightly.

Bleach.

Nolan tosses the bottle in the recycling bin and then

stands and faces the doorway to the house and looks down the hallway. The green light from the alarm clock flashes regularly across the floor of Cosmo's room, reflected on the synthetic wood flooring.

Nolan walks down the hallway toward his brother's room but stops at the door to Cosmo's office. Closed. Always closed. Nolan wraps his hand around the knob and he turns it and gently pushes against the door, but it's locked.

—Hello?

　　—Hey.

　　—I don't really have time to talk right now, Nolan.

　　—Then why pick up?

Silence.

Then:

　　—What do you want?

　　—I just wanted to tell you that I lied about going to the hospital.

　　—I don't know what you're talking about.

　　—I told you about the guy I worked with, the one who set himself on fire.

　　—Yeah.

　　—I told you I went to the hospital—

　　—But you didn't.

　　—No, I went to the hospital, but I lied to you about sitting with his wife. I stood in the door, and she started to cry, and I walked away. I was too ashamed to tell you that.

　　—And that's why you left?

　　—No. That's part of it, but no. Anytime things gets difficult, I pick up and I move on. I've been that way for longer than I care to remember.

—I'm sorry that what we had was difficult for you, Nolan.

—Difficult is the wrong word.

—You should be more careful with your words, then.

—This isn't easy for me, Linda.

—Good.

—I'm trying to tell you I care about you.

—And I cared about you.

He hears that clearly, what she said.

—Do you think you could care for me again?

—Just a second.

—What?

—Yeah. I'm almost done with this.

—Linda?

—Nolan.

—Is someone there?

—That's none of your business anymore, Nolan.

—I care for you.

Linda sighs. Just as Nolan is about to speak, she says:

—I'm done messing around with guys who are still trying to figure out who they are, Nolan. I'm too old for that.

He hears a voice in the background.

—I have to go, she says. I have plans.

She hangs up on him. Nolan hangs up the phone himself and he stands there for a second before he punches the chrome change box, hard, at the bottom of the pay phone. The flap on the change return slot clanks once, but the sound reverberates in his ear, it rings in the sharp pain that runs from his knuckles into his forearm.

Cosmo and Nolan drive Eastside Road on the Fourth of July,

heading north on their return to Burnridge from a structure fire that took place the day before.

A string of one-room cottages, old farmworkers' housing that had been bought by a firm out of Marin and were scheduled to be remodeled and turned into vacation rentals, burned to their concrete pier foundations. Old concrete, Nolan noticed when they got there, mixed with river pebbles probably harvested on site back when the land around them was prune orchard or hop fields.

They drove out to the fire because Cosmo wanted to see the scene and because Nolan liked the idea of the ride. When they arrived at the destroyed cottages an insurance adjuster was standing in the shade of several tall oaks that were badly burned by the fire but not totally destroyed. Cosmo showed the man his press pass he'd kept hold of and that was the only conversation between them. The man left shortly after, and Nolan and Cosmo stayed to survey the damage and then left themselves.

On the ride back to Burnridge, at the quiet intersection of Eastside Road and Old Redwood Highway, they come to a stop.

—Shit, Nolan says.

—What? Cosmo lifts his chin in the direction of the young hitchhiker standing along the side of the road. You know him?

Before Nolan can answer, Mace, having noticed Nolan's hat, saunters over to the Valiant. He places his hands on the passenger-side windowsill, inches from Nolan, and bends at the waist to bring his suntanned face down to the opening.

—Fancy meeting you here. He smiles, and dark flecks of chewing tobacco show in the lines between his teeth.

—You need a ride? Nolan asks.

—Is a pig's ass pork?

—Ha, Cosmo exclaims. Climb in.

On the three-mile drive back to Burnridge, Mason sits in the backseat with his arms outstretched at either side of him, his head turned to one side to look out the window at the passing countryside, and his chin up, challenging the wind that blows in his face. Nolan can sense the kid's about to talk. He can sense it's only a matter of time before he or Cosmo opens their mouths and the car fills with conversation.

—You all going to the fireworks, tonight? Mason says finally.

—I'm thinking about it, Cosmo responds. What about you?

—Oh, hell, yes.

—Down at the high school?

—Fuck that mob. Best place to watch is from Reservoir Ridge.

—I prefer the golf course.

Mason thinks about this.

—Number five green?

—Seven fairway.

—Hmm, I might have to check that out.

Nolan bites the inside of his lip and breathes out through his nose. He keeps his face turned to his window. Mason says:

—Back in the day, the ninth tee box would have been choice.

—Is that where the water tanks are? Cosmo asks.

—Now, there's the spot. Mason nods. Climb up on one of those fuckers.

Cosmo slows the Valiant as they close upon a spectrum of colorfully dressed bicyclists riding the shoulder.

—There's got to be twenty grand in equipment right there, Cosmo says.

—At least, Mason agrees.

—You ride?

—Only when they run on gasoline.

Nolan sets his jaw and shakes his head slightly.

—How do you two know each other? Mason asks Cosmo.

—Brothers. Cosmo points his thumb at Nolan and then at himself.

—You never said anything about having a brother in town. Mason swats Nolan's shoulder.

—The rambler here is adopted, Cosmo responds.

—Seriously? Mason asks.

—He's joking, Nolan says.

Cosmo passes the cyclists and accelerates the Valiant.

—You in the trades, too? Mason asks Cosmo.

—No, I write for the *Observer*. Or I did.

—What's your byline?

—Cosmo Swift.

Mason jolts forward, leaning into the space between Nolan and his brother.

—*The* Cosmo Swift?

—You're familiar with my work.

—Hell, yes, I am.

Mason reaches over the seat and offers Cosmo his hand, which Cosmo takes. They shake.

—Mason Drove, the kid says. Pleasure to meet you.

—You, too.

—You've been covering the fires.

—I was.

—Not anymore?

—Not anymore.

—What happened?

—Can't say. Confidentiality agreement.

—Damn. Mason sits back and stretches out his arms. Grandma is going to be disappointed. She loves your stuff. Has me run out to buy her copy Wednesday night each week from the same newsstand. "No point in waiting until Thursday for them to deliver it if it's available in the box on Wednesday," she says.

Nolan focuses on the vineyards, holding one vine in his gaze until the Valiant passes it and then immediately picking up another in hopes that he can disappear into his concentration.

—You live out this way? Cosmo asks Mason.

—My family's been in this valley four generations. We're old Californians. How long you been here?

—Only since 2000.

—Welcome.

—Thank you.

—Writer and thinker like you. Shit, Grandma's going to flip when I tell her who gave me a ride to town.

Cosmo grabs the wheel with his left hand so he can nudge Nolan with his right elbow. Nolan just shakes his head and follows the vines. Cosmo settles in his seat, a smile on his face.

—You ever think about starting a blog? Mason asks.

—The thought has crossed my mind.

—You tell your adopted brother here when you do to be sure and tell me. Me and Grandma are going to be your first subscribers.

A string of fires are set in quick succession in the days that immediately follow. One man reports standing at his kitchen window, washing the last of his dinner dishes, when a shadowy figure runs from his neighbor's trash can, which was rolled down to the curb for pick-up the next morning. Moments after the figure disappears in the dark, the can catches fire, the flames tall enough to reach the leaves of a Gravenstein apple, loaded with ripening fruit. More than a dozen fires are set in cans throughout the town that night, each one with the lid thrown back and the contents doused with gasoline.

The next afternoon, a mother taking her children to the playground reports arriving to find several redwood picnic tables pushed to the end of a concrete footpad, where the heat from the flames is enough to melt the slide of a plastic play structure.

Two nights later, an elderly woman receives a knock at her front door around midnight. She opens the door to find a trail of fire leading down her walkway and into the street. The trail converges with several other trails, all leading down from neighbors' front doors, into an illuminated gyre drawn in diesel at the center of the street. When the woman looks around, several other neighbors are opening their doors or already standing in their own doorways, watching the flames die out.

A television news crew arrives in town and posts up in front of city hall. They follow the police and fire department during the day, but with city hall as their backdrop, they send out their evening dispatches, complete with interviews of opinionated locals, transplants, and tourists, cut with footage of the neighborhood-watch programs that have sprung up across the town, men and women wearing reflector vests and armed with flashlights, cell phones, and fire extinguishers. At all hours, now, Cosmo tells Nolan, residents are walking the streets hoping to catch the arsonist in the act.

—My guess, Cosmo says, is he's among them. He's hiding in plain sight.

One morning, while Nolan is tying his lunch to the handlebars of the ten-speed in the driveway, Cosmo pulls in and climbs out of the car, notepad in hand and camera dangling against his chest. He was out all night, he tells Nolan, because:

—Someone needs to watch the watchers.

Several hours after sunset the day following, five large bonfires are lit on Veterans' Memorial Beach, near the river, in a neat row. Onlookers gather across the river and traffic slows on the two-lane steel bridge to watch the firefighters extinguish and break apart the piles of giant reed, cut down nearby and built up on the gravel beach. But, as the final fire is broken apart, the firefighters' radios chirp, and they run up to their trucks and, sirens blaring, race southwest to the outskirts of town where a house that was under construction – the first new home targeted by the arsonist – is burning to the ground.

—The bonfires were a diversion, Cosmo tells Nolan later that night. He's toying with them. Even the tourists are here now for the spectacle.

Production on the film, disrupted while the set makers rebuilt the façade down on the plaza that had been destroyed by fire, is underway again, but with a 24/7 security detail on site that is also protecting other locations where filming was scheduled to take place.

—Hollywood wanted to film here because our town looks like the thing they imagine. They imagine quaint. Bucolic. Provincial. But what they got was insurrection. Hell, what they got was terrorism.

—This isn't terrorism, Cosmo.

—I disagree. Besides, wait and see what they charge this guy with when they catch him, bud. You'll see.

The next morning, a jogger reports coming upon a telephone pole set afire. She notices it as she crests the hill, and just as she realizes what it is, an old car races past her, and a man gets out and starts taking pictures of it. Then, he just climbs back in his car and drives away.

—I couldn't decide which was stranger, the jogger tells one of the TV reporters for the evening news. The fire, or the man photographing it. I still can't.

—You know, Mace says, studying the end of his cigarette. This is about as good as it gets.

Nolan lies with his hat lowered over his brow, his hands folded on his chest.

—I read once, Mace says, that they used to fight bulls and bears in this valley here. The Spanish did. Mexifornians, or whatever they were. They built these big old rings and just threw them in it.

Nolan keeps his eyelids shut, breathing in the smell of his own sweaty hatband.

—Can you imagine a fucking bear tearing at a bull like that? Hella señoritas all hanging around, crying and shit?

Nolan concentrates on his breathing.

—Did you know that this valley is as far south as the Russian Empire got and as far north as the Spanish did? This is No Man's Land, here. Bulls-and-bears territory. Did you know that?

Nolan doesn't answer him.

—Joe's taking his sweet time, huh? Probably noshing all that free lumber-yard popcorn. Probably stashing it in that sling of his. You think he's milking that sling business?

Mace stubs out his cigarette against the heel of his boot.

—I read that bulls-and-bears shit in school. I read everything they put in front of me and then some. I'm a straight
scholar, like that. My problem is I can't sit still. Those walls
can't contain me.

He flicks the stub out into the trash heap and settles
back against Guillermo's two-by-ten. While tapping another
cigarette from the soft pack he keeps buttoned in the front
pocket of his shirt, several fall loose on the porch.

—Man down, the kid says.

Nolan lifts his hat to see the cigarettes scattered there,
skinny and white. He sees that Mace doesn't move to put
them back in the pack but begins to finger them around the
porch boards.

—I don't miss school one bit, though, Mason says, lighting
the cigarette in his mouth, and then arranging the ones he's
spilled. No, siree, Bob. In fact, I'm glad they kicked me out.
This is my Harvard and Yale, you know. Get on with my real
education. Establish myself.

Nolan sets his molars against one another. Almost as an
aside, Mason says:

—Nah, Joe's all right, as far as popcorn-munchers go.

Then, reaching up to pick tobacco from his lip:

—I ever tell you why they kicked me out of school in the
first place? They said I missed too many days, which is bullshit,
because I for sure stopped by at least once every day to see a
couple special young ladies I happen to know. A few, in fact.
But then I went and got put up in juvie.

He digs soggy white-bread remnants from the upper
narrows of his teeth. He looks at the wet, white masticated
mass at the end of his finger and then flicks it in the direction
of the trash heap.

—I was working at this hotel downtown, me and some other dudes I went to school with. They dared me to piss in this one suitcase and say it was *agua*. We were always messing with the tourists and shit. Bunch of assholes acting like our backyard's their playground. Just coming up here to show off their cars and watches and shit. The judge said what I'd done was willful and malicious. I volunteered to go to Iraq, but they wouldn't take me at sixteen. Dude whose suitcase it was, he fought me in the lobby. I have to give the man that. Never did find out what part of the country he was from.

Mace uncrosses and crosses his ankles, his heels heavy on the porch boards. Nolan can hear him pushing the cigarettes around, doing something with them.

—When I was kicking it in juvie, some counselor decided I should be in the loony bin. The thing about the loony bin, though, is there's nothing to do there but mess with the crazies.

Nolan can feel Mason thriving on his silence, the tension it holds.

—There was this one girl there. My age. This rich-ass slut from Marin. Everyone there was nuts. Literally. But she wasn't, either. She just liked playing tough and talking dirty, but I called her on it my first day. We got to be pretty tight, me and her. We'd slip off now and then and share a bullet, laugh at the retards. I straight up told her one day, you talk shit in these groups and all, but you're full of it. She got all hangdog on me after that, so I said, come on, and patted my hip. More I kept telling her she was full of it, more she had to prove she wasn't. People are fucked that way.

—Anyhow, Mason says after a second or two, we'd sit around in a circle with the crazies, all medicated and drooling down their bibs, and she'd get to blubbering about Daddy this and Mommy that, and I'd pretend to nod off. I even fell asleep for reals once. Snored hella loud. When the counselor woke me up, the retards were all red-faced and laughing and shit, but she got all mad and stormed out, and this stupid-ass counselor said, "Now, Mason." Now, Mason.

He is using both hands to arrange the cigarettes now, the one in his mouth sending a thin wisp of smoke up into his eye, causing him to squint.

—But we had some fun, too, grab ass and kissing. I even gave her a hickey on her tit once so no one'd know. But she kept holding out on me. Said she might use again, or kill herself, but no way was she going to let someone do her until it meant something. So I just started ignoring her. Didn't even look in her direction when she came up all crying and grabbing for my hand. Wasn't too long after that she came up saying she hella wanted to. So we slipped off for a bullet, and I did her in the stairwell.

Nolan's eyes are open. He stares at the inside of his hat, the sunlight shattering through the spaces in the weave.

—I heard she went nuts after that. Took some pills or some shit.

Nolan sits up and adjusts his hat.

—Didn't even wrap my tool. I could have a disease or some shit.

—Or a kid, Nolan says, and Mason laughs and slaps his leg.

—I never even thought of that.

Nolan sits up and rests his hat back on his head and then cants it forward.

—Back to work? the kid asks.

—Yep.

—Let's do it.

And that's when Nolan sees it. The kid has constructed a house with the cigarettes. Four verticals, four horizontals, and four diagonals to complete the hipped roof. With the lit cigarette in his mouth, Mace holds the flame from his lighter to one vertical and then to another, setting the tiny structure on fire.

10

The doorbell rings. With Cosmo typing in his office, Nolan opens the front door, where a young woman stands before him holding a bottle of chilled white wine.

—Hey, she says, placing her sunglasses on her head and then extending her hand. I'm Maxine.

—Nolan.

—You're the nomad brother who lives in the garage.

—Afraid so.

—Nice to meet you.

—You, too.

—Smells delicious.

—Thank you.

—I didn't know you were going to be here for dinner.

—I'm on my way out.

—He didn't tell you about me, did he?

—Sure he did.

—Right. She smiles. That him typing?

—Yeah.

—Can I come in?

—Of course. I'm sorry.

Maxine steps forward and tugs playfully at the end of the dishtowel lying flat against Nolan's chest.

—Cute, she says. You'll make some lucky fella a nice wifey someday.

The typing stops.

—Partner, Cosmo yells from behind the door, is that Maxine?

—Yes, Cosmo, it's me.

—Tell her I'll be right there. I'm almost done with this chapter.

—I can hear you fine, Cosmo.

Nolan is about to turn toward the kitchen when Maxine places her hand lightly on his forearm. There's a weight to her touch that he's felt before, and while he doesn't mind it in that moment, it's not something he would ever act on.

—Hey, she whispers, coming in close enough so that he can smell her perfume, subtle and elegant and sophisticated, have you ever seen the inside of his office?

—Can't say that I have.

—He keeps the door locked.

Nolan looks her in the eye. She smiles and says:

—But you probably already knew that.

—Can't say that I did.

Nolan turns and walks to the kitchen. Maxine follows him but stops at the center of the living room, her purse over her shoulder, the bottle of wine at her side. He can feel her watching him as he folds the dishtowel over the oven handle, takes up a pearl-button dress shirt from the back of a chair, puts it on, and begins snapping the buttons.

—You don't want to stay and eat what you cooked? she asks.

—No, I got someplace to be.

—I could call a friend.

—Tell Cosmo to pull the chicken from the oven in twenty or it'll dry out.

—Can't have that, now, can we?

Nolan lifts his chin in the direction of the bottle of wine she's holding.

—Do me a favor?

—Name it.

—Make sure he eats some before you all get too far into that.

—Aye aye, Captain.

Then, she says:

—You're not going to tell him, are you?

—Tell him what?

She thins her lips and nods, and Nolan turns to leave.

The streets are empty of traffic. The fog has come up the river and cooled the heat of the day. Nolan walks past a basketball hoop, the bottom edge of the clear Plexiglas backboard bearing smudges from the ball and grease from fingertips along the bottom edge. Behind it, in one of two second-story windows above a garage, a figure in silhouette holds a wireless video game controller out in front of his waist. Lasers flash on the screen before the figure and an avatar in an imagined future jumps a wildly impossible distance with relative ease. In the bedroom next door, a second television monitor displays the colorful moving tiles of some child's puzzle.

Nolan keeps walking. He heads west and then north. The phone booth in front of the Chinese restaurant is empty. Moths flick at the dome light. Inside the restaurant, a man sits alone in a booth reading the newspaper while eating noodles with a fork. Nolan stands across the street from the restaurant. He watches the waitress set the man's check on the table and the man smiles up at her and she smiles back and then walks away.

Nolan crosses the street, picks up the receiver, and dials in the prepaid number followed by Linda's number.

—Hello? she says.

—I need to talk to you.

—OK?

—What would you do if you think someone's doing something wrong, and you think you might be the only one who knows about it?

—Seriously, Nolan? How old are you right now?

—Don't be mean, Linda. It doesn't suit you.

He hears her set something down and shift the phone from one ear to the other.

—What kind of wrong are we talking about?

—Setting houses on fire.

—The firebug?

—Yeah.

—It's your brother, isn't it?

—No.

—Who, then?

—This kid I work with. I think.

—The one who tells the jokes?

—No, he got deported.

—Deported deported?

—Yeah, he and his brother.

—Jesus. How sad.

—His replacement.

—And you saw him set fire to something?

—No. Well, yes, but no.

—I'm confused. Did you, or did you not?

—No.

—Did he tell you he's the firebug?

—In so many words.

—But you don't actually know for sure he's starting fires.

—No.

—Then there's nothing to do, is there?

—He's Joe's nephew.

—Who's Joe?

—The contractor I work for.

—So tell Joe. Or Homeland Security. I don't know. Stay out of it.

—I don't want anyone getting hurt.

—Unless you know for certain, Nolan, unless you've seen him do it or he's confessed, I don't see that there's anything you can do.

—Yeah, I hear you.

Nolan reaches up and touches the wall of the phone booth, and the glass steams around his fingertips.

—Is any of this true, Linda asks, or are you just doing this to call me?

—Both.

—Listen, tell Joe you're suspicious of the kid. Take it to the family. That's the least you can do.

Joe lives in a 1970s ranch house several miles east of Burnridge. The one-story structure sits on five acres of grasses that Joe mows every other week during the summer months with the aid of a three-horsepower rider-mower, a cooler of cold beer, and a fat joint. A seasonal creek delineates the length of the southern property line, and lying on the other side of this line, a hillside of buckeye and oak and an outcrop of serpentine, mantled in blue-green and orange lichen. The other three sides of the property give way to hundreds upon hundreds of acres of vineyard.

When Nolan rides up the driveway, he finds Joe at the center of a partially mowed field, working on the mower's steering column. The contractor wears flip-flops and a faded T-shirt bearing the advertisement of a surfing apparel company. Old heaps of rusted farm equipment line the driveway. The leaves on the buckeyes have begun to yellow. The hillsides resemble tinder.

—You found the place, Joe says, setting an open-ended wrench in his sling. He wipes his hand on his blue jeans and he and Nolan shake hands.

—Beer? he offers.

—Please.

Joe opens the cooler, bungeed to the back of the mower, and inside of it are six empties.

—Looks like everyone's been over twice. Let's go up to the house.

They enter the house through a door that opens to the kitchen. Joe's wife is sitting on the couch in the living room reading a picture book to their son, Joey. The boy grasps an action figure in his hand.

—Sweetheart, Joe says, his head in the fridge, this is Nolan. Nolan, Maria, my wife.

Nolan removed his hat when he entered the house, and now he steps into the living room and extends his free hand.

—Nice to meet you.

—You, too.

—This is Joey, she says. Can you say hello to Nolan, Joey?

The boy buries his face against his mother's arm, and his action figure dangles by the ankles.

—We'll be out front, Joe says.

They sit in the shade on the cool brick steps that lead up to the front door. The day is hot and dry. Cumulonimbus clouds tower above a mountain lake to the northeast. The bottom portions of the cloud blur into blue. Nolan can see the circular outlines on the brick steps of where Maria's pots were arranged. The steps have been swept and washed, but traces of the flower pots remain faint on the bricks, dark still in the grout.

—What's eating your mind? Joe says.

Nolan looks down into the mouth of the beer can.

—I got concerns about Mace.

Joe blows out his cheeks and exhales.

—Here I thought you were going to jump ship on me.

—I said I wouldn't.

Joe raises his beer can between them in a dismissive gesture.

—Kid lies through his teeth.

—That may be true, but there's something about how he lies that disturbs me.

—He just watches too much television, bro. Too many video games and all that. That generation doesn't understand there's no reset button.

Nolan sets the beer can on the step beside him. He begins massaging the calluses along the top of his left palm with the side of his right index finger, sliding his left hand back and forth over the top of his right.

—I'm not sure that's all it is.

—He's a temporary fix.

—All I'm saying is I think someone ought to keep a watchful eye on him. Who knows what he's liable to get up to when we're looking the other way?

—OK. Will do.

Nolan pries at Joe's eyes and the contractor smiles.

—What? Joe asks.

—I'm just saying.

—No, man, I hear you. I do. Loud and clear. I'll keep an eye on the little dude.

They sit in silence, looking out over the partially mowed field, at the dry creek across the way and the lichen-covered rocks up the hill. Joe sips from his beer.

—Must've come up for the water, Nolan says, raising his can toward the hills.

—What's that?

—Your rattler. With the drought and all, he must've come up to your wife's plants for the water.

—I talked to Joe, Nolan says into the phone, just as a truck, laden with foreign-made cars, rumbles past.

—What'd he say?

—I told him I had concerns about the kid's behavior.

—But you didn't mention the fires.

—No.

—Why not?

—As it was, he didn't believe me.

—I wouldn't want to either.

—You think I should have come out and said it, though?

—If you're wrong, it makes you look bad, but if you're right, and you don't come out and say it directly, in the long run it makes him look bad because his nephew is an arsonist.

—Shit.

—Right.

—I just wish I had some evidence.

—That's when you go directly to the authorities.

Nolan massages his forehead and sighs. Linda says:

—You were right to at least mention your concerns to Joe. He was probably dismissive because he's embarrassed. Wouldn't you be?

—I guess. Yeah.

A second of silence passes between the former lovers. Hoping not to lose her, Nolan speaks abruptly and without thinking:

—You know, you ever want to fly up here one of these weekends for a visit, I'll buy the ticket.

—Where'd that come from?

—I was just thinking we could drive out to the ocean, spend a few days there. Maybe run down to the city for a night. There's a small airport, not far from here. They got direct flights to and from Vegas. I might be able to get a day off if you want to extend your weekend, even.

—Nolan.

—Just think about it.

—Nolan, I've started dating again.

—Is it serious?

—No, but apparently we weren't serious either, remember?

—Are you sleeping with him?

—That's none of your business, but you know what, yeah, I am.

Nolan doesn't respond.

—You left, Nolan. You mailed me a fucking letter that said take care, and you left. You actually wrote, "Take care."

—I know it.

—I'm not coming up there to see you, Nolan. And I don't think we should talk like this anymore. I don't think it's good for you.

—Linda.

—Don't. OK? Just stop.

While sinking sixteens into blocks for the transom they're installing above the bedroom doors upstairs, Nolan smashes his thumb with the waffled face of his framing hammer. The pain is excruciating, and his thumb, bleeding around the fingernail, immediately begins to throb. Nolan climbs down from the ladder, drops his hammer in its holster, and wraps his thumb tightly in his handkerchief.

He stands for a moment, watching his blood soak through the white cotton. Then, he hangs his bags on a nail in a stud he put there for that purpose and walks downstairs to the living room, where the site's first aid kit is stored. He finds Joe standing in the shadows to the side of a window. He's spying on Mason while the kid, in the back of Joe's Ram, rummages through diamond-treaded tool boxes. Joe waves Nolan over.

—Look at this, he says mischievously.

—What's he doing?

—I told him to get me the board stretcher.

Mason has his head buried beneath the tool-box lid.

—Look at him, Joe says, almost squealing. He's been out there for ten minutes.

—He'll probably be out there ten more.

Joe notices Nolan's thumb.

—You all right?

—Not paying attention to what I was doing.

Then, looking at his hand, Nolan stammers:

—Joe, I—

But Joe interrupts him:

—Look, look.

He smacks Nolan on the shoulder and points to Mason, who holds up a four-foot level in one hand and a come-along in the other.

—Oh, yeah, Joe laughs, he's nothing but trouble.

11

Nolan sits on the love seat in the garage, the nails laid out on the road atlas next to him. His thumb is still throbbing. He cleaned it in the shower and the bandage is fresh and white and almost glowing against the brown glass of his beer bottle, against the tan of his hand.

The garage door is open and a breeze comes up the driveway, bringing with it the cool of the evening's marine layer. A mourning dove coos from the power line that dips toward the garage roof. The house is quiet despite Cosmo being home as well.

Nolan's mind drifts over the map until he arrives at his decision. Once the roof is off the farmhouse and the trusses are rolled and sheathed, he'll leave; he'll give Joe two weeks. He wanted to tell him as much this afternoon, but he didn't. Also, he'll need to tell Cosmo soon.

He needs to tell his brother now.

Nolan sets the empty bottle on the concrete floor of the garage and stands and walks into the house. Standing outside the office door, Nolan listens for a second or two to the quiet on the other side before he taps lightly on the jamb with a knuckle of his middle finger.

—Hey, bud, he says, you got a sec?

He taps once more and waits for a response that does not come, so he reaches down and turns the knob.

Nolan finds Cosmo lying on a blanket on the floor, facing the wall. He is curled up in the fetal position with a pillow over his head and a thin blanket covering him. The walls in the room are covered with index cards, thumbtacked in place and partially obscuring a collection of maps of Russia and Japan. Naval charts show through from behind the cards. Mercator and Peters maps, too. Tied to the thumbtacks, to pins in the maps and charts, a plexus of string fills the space of the room, each strand connecting the writing on one index card to one or more cards on the same wall or to other walls of the room. Suspended in the middle of the room, a dense confluence of linking knots concocts an intricate web, beneath which Cosmo sleeps. On a small writing desk, next to a laptop computer, stands a portrait of Cosmo and his ex-wife.

The room's only window is cracked open, and when Nolan opened the door, a light cross-breeze fluttered the blinds and strings. He looks through the swaying network of links and nodes. Snatches of conversations he and Cosmo have had during his stay return to him. He no longer thinks Cosmo is connected to the arsons, but this display of his thinking is unsettling. The cards on the wall are filled with handwriting in blue and black ink, in red and green scrawl. The thumbtacks and pins appear to be color-coded references themselves, all of it a labyrinth of references.

A bookshelf, beside the desk, houses dozens of composition notebooks. One of the notebooks is opened flat and Nolan can see the pages are filled with handwriting that runs horizontally, vertically, and/or diagonally. Writing almost overlapping writing, but not quite. He sees what must be Cosmo's manuscript standing three reams tall on a nightstand in the corner, a fist-sized piece of obsidian on top of it to serve as a paper weight.

In the upper reaches of the room, gossamer strands connect to the string web, connect to the web and to the skip-troweled ceiling, where they blend into the eggshell-white paint. Nolan studies Cosmo, lying on the floor, a book beside him, the page heavily underlined and highlighted, filled with marginalia. The corner of the thin blanket is draped over a heap of Russian-language tapes carefully stacked beside a kanji chart. The largest map in the room is filled with curves and lines, the words *Strait of Tsushima* covered with routes taken. Another map illustrates the calculus of a lopsided battle. Across the room from this, a world map shows the long, arduous route the Baltic Fleet took to get to the strait, with lengths of string running out from pins along the way to chapters and paragraphs and sentences written on the cards, to individual words even: *Rare Earths, Comic Books, Da Nang, Jazz, BRIC, Quilting, The Gold Rush, Dad*. Letters and words in the expanding and contracting narrative, a web of Cosmo's own making.

Nolan watches his brother sleep. Not far from the ends of his fingers rests a ball of string and a pair of scissors, pointed blade against blunt blade, held fast by a slotted pivot pin. The quiet of the room, punctuated by the occasional fluttering of the cards in the breeze, makes space for a steady thrumming in Nolan's ears even after he closes the door, even after he returns to his place in the garage.

With all the termite damage to the trusses, Mace and Nolan tear off the composite roofing and the sheathing in two days.

Then, working from ladders positioned in the upstairs bedrooms, Joe has Mason take down the cords and rafters by the end of the week. For several days the old house stands without a roof, the rooms filled with sunlight, just tall walls giving way to blue sky.

One morning, in the cool of the fog, three wire-bound truss stacks are craned up off the bed of a delivery truck and hoisted to spots atop the farmhouse, from where they will be distributed. The rafter tails rest on opposing top plates, their peaks braced from below with gusseted posts that Nolan had Mace fashion the day prior from plywood scraps and two-by-fours. Before climbing up to walk the top plate, Nolan stops beside a ladder in the master bedroom and takes off his boots and socks. Mace watches him from above, already eager to tackle the dangerous work.

—I got time for a smoke while you bone the dog?

Nolan doesn't respond.

—No, seriously. What the hell are you doing?

—Easier to feel the plate this way.

Mace picks his steps carefully along the top plate over to one of the truss stacks. He sits down and starts pulling off his own boots, one palm cupping the heel, the other wrestling the toe.

—What the fuck are you two doing? Joe asks when he sees the two of them taking off their shoes.

—Tricks of the trade, Mace says, letting his cowboy boots drop to the floor below. Jackson here's part Mohawk.

—The fuck you know about Mohawks? Joe asks.

—I know lots you know you don't know I know.

—I'm not going to waste time trying to figure out if that even makes sense.

While Joe and Mason argue, Nolan places his right foot on the bottom rung of the ladder and both hands on either side of it. He draws a deep breath and exhales slowly in an attempt to gather his thoughts and distance himself from distraction, for rolling trusses two stories up is dangerous work that requires great concentration and skill, and if he falls, he's better off dying, better for him and for his family, who've never counted on him, and on whom he doesn't want to be a burden.

—Hell, Mason says, his voice cracking, Journeyman here keeps imparting knowledge like this barefoot shit, I'm all you're going to need around here before long, Joe.

—As long as I can pay you the same rate.

—Yeah, I been meaning to talk to you about that.

Nolan climbs the ladder.

—Let's get to work, he says stiffly.

—Dollar waiting on a dime here.

They work together, Nolan and Mason, two stories up, carrying one truss at a time out to layout while the peak dangles into the room below, and the inverted rafter tails point over the sides of the farmhouse. They set the truss down on the top plate, and they begin swinging the truss lightly, until, *one*, they force it away, *two*, pull it back, and *three*, with Joe pushing the peak up from below with a length of two-by-four, they roll it into place.

One by one, they carry each truss out and roll it into place and pull it plumb. After nailing it fast to the top plate with vinyl-dipped sixteens, Nolan holds the truss as steady as he can while Mace shimmies out from the previous one and tacks the one they just rolled down with duplex eights driven into a flimsy length of one-by already marked with layout identical to that of the top plate.

—*Dos cabezas*, Mace says, pulling duplex nails from his

pouch. I heard a Mexican at the hardware store call them that.

—Stay focused, Nolan responds.

—You're no fun.

—This isn't supposed to be fun.

—You're boring.

—Better to be boring than injured or dead.

After putting each truss in place, they walk the length of the rooms by way of the narrow top plates, carefully making their way back to the depleting stack with their arms raised to stay balanced above a dangerous fall on either side. Mason beats Nolan back to the stack each time.

—Day's only so long, old man, he says, spitting over the edge of the building and leaning after the spit, pretending that he is about to fall, but catching himself and watching the amorphous, tobacco-laced globs fall.

Nolan stops at the middle of the wall, nothing to reach for but a substantial fall in all directions, and he looks Mason in the eye for a few seconds until the kid says:

—What did I do?

Nolan looks ahead and lifts his hands and outstretches his arms. Then, he slowly raises his chin and looks up at the sky, vast and empty, the set trusses lined up behind him like exposed ribs of some great leviathan, wind scoured and sun bleached. He stands there for some time, his arms outstretched, his face to the sky, his frame held in perfect balance.

When he gets back to the stack, Mace says:

—What was that all about?

—Try it.

Mace starts out along the top plate.

—Try back there first, Nolan says. Someplace where you won't fall and kill yourself.

—I'm all right.

—Mason, Nolan says, the name foreign on his tongue for as familiar it's become to his mind. Just this once, do as I ask.

—Whatever.

Mace returns to the stack. He lifts his hands and stretches out his arms and raises his chin and looks up at the sky and immediately he begins to wobble.

—Damn, he laughs, catching himself on the stack, that's hard as fuck.

Their father rarely spoke about Vietnam and never about combat, never to Nolan, at least. The one or two times Nolan asked his father about the war before he was old enough to realize that his father didn't want to share or to discuss his experiences, his father simply smiled at Nolan, looked him directly in the eye, tousled his hair, and said:

—I don't want to talk about that, bud.

Nolan was pretty sure Cosmo had gotten the same response, but that didn't stop his brother from telling a group of friends that their father had crawled through tunnels with a .45 and shot Viet Cong soldiers dead. Chance had gotten this image from a movie he and Nolan snuck into after their mother had dropped them off at the theater to see a movie about a talking duck from outer space. They'd both wanted to see the movie about the war but they knew better than to ask to see it, so, after consulting the newspaper, they made their plan.

The experience changed Nolan's conception of his father and Chance's conception of himself.

When word got back to their father that Chance was making up stories about his experience in Vietnam and that they had snuck into the R-rated film, their father sat them down on the couch in the living room one night and sat in a chair opposite them. A fire burned in the fireplace behind him. In a calm, patient voice, he said:

—You want to know what Vietnam was like?

—No, Chance answered, looking at his hands in his lap.

—Then why did you sneak into that movie?

—I don't know, Chance said.

—Nolan?

—I don't know, Nolan said.

Their father sighed.

—Do you want me to tell you what Vietnam was like?

Chance nodded.

—Nolan?

—Yes, he said.

—Can either of you still see those men and the fire?

Chance's lower lip was quivering. Nolan nodded.

—Yes, he said.

—It was kind of like that. But a lot of that.

—Why did you volunteer, then? Chance asked.

—I thought it was the right thing to do.

Chance was crying now. He wasn't sobbing, but his breathing was erratic. Their father placed a hand on the boy's knee.

—Do you still think that way? Nolan asked.

—Sometimes yes, and sometimes no.

—When do you think yes?

—When I think of you two.

—When do you not think it? Chance interjected.

—When I think of you two.

Years later, when Nolan was studying the war in the eighth grade, he asked his mother about his father's experience and she told him that he didn't want to talk about it with him or his brother because he was a private man, and his privacy was to be respected.

When Nolan asked her if he'd been drafted, she said:

—No, he volunteered.

—Why?

—Because he was young and idealistic.

—What does idealistic mean?

—Really? she asked.

But seeing she'd made him self-conscious of his early struggles with words, despite her education and Chance's faculty for the English language, she said:

—He came from a class of people who think they are above service. He thought they were wrong to think that way, so, to make a point, he volunteered.

—Did he kill people?

—You have to ask him to answer that.

—He doesn't want to talk about it.

—Then you have to respect that.

Nolan was quiet.

—I still don't know what idealistic means.

His mother smiled at him.

—Go look it up, she said.

Cosmo and Nolan sit in a booth at the local pizza parlor. Nolan stares at a stainless fork he's turning on the glossy veneer tabletop while biting at the inside of his cheek. Cosmo sits across from him, leaning back against the wood-paneled booth, his hands behind his head, in his hair. Chili flakes and grated Parmesan have been swept under the napkin dispenser between them. Cosmo adjusts his glasses and begins to gesture as he speaks:

—The thing about conspiracy theories is that they relieve us of personal accountability. They provide the scapegoat. The theory itself becomes a secular god. We forget our history. We submit to a higher power. They're convenient.

Nolan wipes the table, his eyes lingering where the dampness of his hand leaves swipe marks on the surface. He waits for the moment when he can slip a word in edgewise.

—Stone. Bronze. Iron. Plastic. Silicon. Wireless. But what if that's it?

There's a fervor to Cosmo's latest rant, a passion that makes Nolan wonder if Cosmo's been drinking earlier in the day than usual.

—I unplugged my computer at work one day, and the electricity arced and it was as if I was looking into the eye of a sleeping Cyclops, suddenly awake.

Two boys run past the brothers on their way to a video-game booth at the back of the pizza parlor. A young woman's voice, mutilated by a loudspeaker, says:

—Ernesto? Order ready for Ernest?

Members of a co-ed softball team sit at the large round table in the front window of the parlor. Outside, the sun-drenched parking lot slots are filled with automobiles, heat visibly radiating off their roofs and hoods. A few starlings hop and peck at the asphalt, hop and peck.

Cosmo continues:

—I don't know. Maxine's crazy. When she's hot, she's hot; when she's not, she's not. You say something she disagrees with, but has no counterargument for, other than she knows she's being irrational, and that's fine, because screw you for caring. Caring means you're weak. It's all posturing. Constant posturing. Are we that self-aware now? Is that what thirty-five-hundred-odd years of Moses David Jesus Hamlet has left us with? Spoiled rotten with indecision?

Cosmo sits with his back to the order/pick-up counter, where a man who is not wearing a shirt stands tucking a tall stack of plastic glasses under his armpit. The boy who accompanies him stands on tiptoes, peeking into the salad bar, both hands cupped over the edge of the glossy countertop.

—Come here, Nolan hears the shirtless man say to the boy.

Cosmo says:

—How much time do you dedicate to considering the potential flaws in your thinking?

—What? Nolan asks.

—This is the beauty of our culture, but it can also be debilitating to the point of paralysis, metaphorically and intellectually, but maybe it's also motivational? I can't tell anymore. It's just everything at once and I'm never the same.

The shirtless man walks past the booth where Nolan and Cosmo sit, carrying the glasses under his arm and two large pizzas out in front of him. The boy follows carrying a pitcher of bright orange, artificially colored soda. He stares into the liquid, using its surface to gauge each step. As they pass the booth, Nolan says:

—I saw your office, Cosmo.

But Cosmo does not hear Nolan.

—Look at this. Cosmo raises his hands, palms up and fingers spread. I mean, hey, buddy, put on a shirt, for crying out loud. This is a family place.

The shirtless man stops and turns.

—What?

—Put on a shirt, dude.

The man sets the pizzas down on the table of an empty booth and puts down the glasses, still beaded wet from the dishwashing machine. Nolan watches the boy nervously watch the orange soda.

—What'd you say? the man asks Cosmo.

—Come on, man, this is a family place. Put on a shirt.

The man repositions his feet so as to brace his core. He throws his chin at Cosmo:

—Make me, bro.

Cosmo closes his mouth and shakes his head.

—That's what I thought, the man says.

Cosmo smirks.

—Please. Put. On. A. Shirt.

The man turns away:

—Whatever.

Cosmo slams his fist down on the table, rattling the condiment jars and the napkin dispenser. The boy carrying the pitcher of orange soda startles and spills at the sudden burst of sound. People in the parlor look in Cosmo's direction.

—No, Cosmo yells. This is not "whatever," man.

—Easy, Cosmo, Nolan mutters.

—There is no "whatever," bro. There are always consequences. No man is an island because all islands are connected beneath the ocean.

Cosmo lunges out of the booth and shoves the man in the chest with both hands. As the man staggers back, Nolan slides out of his seat with his back to the man, who rights himself and draws back his fist. Nolan turns in time with the man's swing, and a colorless flash of pain rams into the back of his skull. The muscles of his shoulders and neck cinch, and the insides of his knees suddenly ache.

—Aw, the man yelps, crumpled over, grabbing his wrist.
Damn.

Nolan puts his hand over his eye. When he feels Cosmo
trying to get around him, he reaches out with his free hand,
wraps his arm around his brother, and holds him close.

—You will not prevail, Cosmo yells. Not on my watch.

By this time Nolan can see the jerseys of the softball team
surrounding them. He can see their socked and sandaled and
cleated feet on the carpeted floor.

—You all right, man? he hears in one ear.

—My wrist, the shirtless man moans. I busted my wrist.

—Take it easy, someone says to Cosmo.

Nolan can feel his brother wrestling against him. He smells
of deodorant sweat. Nolan can feel fingers trying to pry free
the cinch he has on Cosmo's shirt.

—Are you all right? Nolan hears someone say to him again.

—I will stand against you, Cosmo yells.

—Let it go, man, Nolan hears another voice.

—We got him, man. The breath hot in Nolan's ear. You
can let go now, the voice says.

Nolan can feel his cheek swelling below his eye into the
palm of his hand.

—I will stand against you, Cosmo yells again. You and
your barbarous horde.

—We got them, the voice says. Let go.

Nolan releases Cosmo and steps back. With his hand
covering his eye, he looks up and sees Cosmo hauled down
the aisle by two of the softball players. The boy is standing to
the side, the pitcher of orange soda shaking in his hands, slosh-
ing against the rim of the pitcher, running down both hands
and darkening the carpet at the toes of his small feet.

Nolan shoves his way to the front door. Outside, the sun shines brilliantly. He stumbles into traffic but a horn blast sends him staggering back to the sidewalk.

Breathe, he tells himself, seething with anger, his jaw clenched. Breathe.

The air tastes of exhaust and baking pizza. He hears Cosmo running up behind him and he balls his hand into a fist.

—Nolan.

—Leave me alone, Chance.

—Dude, where're you going?

—Home.

—I'll give you a ride.

—I prefer to walk.

—Come on, man.

Nolan stops. He unclenches his fist and splays his fingers at the side of his thigh.

—Chance, I want you to leave me alone.

He doesn't walk home, not directly. At Railroad Park over-looking Memorial Beach, he sits on a bench in the shade with his hand on his eye, silently berating himself for having left Las Vegas in the first place, for having bothered to stop to see Cosmo.

This is why you stay alone. This is why you forsake family. Because for as much as you care for yourself, they care for themselves, and to forget that and to think you can be there for them, that you can help them in some way, will ultimately prove you the fool.

Across the river, the summer beach is filled with sun-bathers. Screaming children frolic in the water or chase each other across the hot sand. Uphill, at the shaded picnic grounds, families set up around barbeque stands, the smell of burning briquettes already in the air. Beneath the automobile bridge, a row of light-blue paddle boats are lashed together, and farther along, near the arsonist's bonfires, overturned aluminum rental canoes shine in the sunlight. A small wooden shack is the only structure on the beach. Sunlight glints off security cameras, positioned at the gable ends, aimed at the canoes and paddle boats. Nolan stares at the black remnants of where the bonfires were lit until a group of boys, yelling and jumping from the girders of the railroad trestle into the river, break his concentration. He looks upstream, where a man in a long-sleeve shirt and dark pants disappears into the giant reeds. The man pushes a bicycle outfitted with panniers. His entire life in those bags, Nolan thinks.

Then:

Your poor mother. Three men in her life and each of you a strain on her selflessness in your own way. Your own self-absorbed, manly way.

He gets up and walks. By sunset, he's standing before the phone booth in front of the Chinese restaurant. The horizon to the west is rimmed with pinks and mauves and the last rays of sunlight brighten a single white spoke of a contrail, dissipating east, into the onset of night. The silver cord dangles from the telephone receiver, which rests in its cradle. The cord loops up and disappears into the black box below the gray, plastic keys but above the chrome change box, with its circular keyhole, black around the edges.

When Nolan leaves a place, it's like when a film ends and the credits roll over a road unfurling before him, and just like that the place disappears from view. Out of sight, out of mind.

But that's not how it is.

A film exists in a contained space, a frame. It has a beginning, a middle, and an end, and thinking that your life is anything like this, that it resembles it in the slightest, is delusional and it only reinforces the illusion of film.

He wants to call Linda. He wants to tell her he was a damn fool and to apologize and to beg her to take him back.

But he doesn't. He can't. Not if he wants her to want to be with him again.

The next day is a Saturday. Two of the four streets bordering the plaza have been cordoned off and a large crowd stands facing the bank façade, a corner of which has been recently repainted so as to conceal the damage done to it by the arsonist. A young woman in a platinum-blond wig sits in the driver's seat of a shiny red convertible parked in front of the bank. She casually smokes a cigarette while a small group of people cluster around her, tending to her hair and makeup. Behind her, and to the side of the bank's front doors, Nolan notices Maxine and another young woman standing arm in arm, laughing self-consciously. They wear cotton summer dresses and their hair has been done up and their faces are covered in makeup.

The sky has been darkening gradually throughout the day as clouds have gathered overhead. Clouds, Nolan notices, not fog, but rain clouds—the first ones he's seen during his stay in Burnridge.

—Places, people, a voice calls through a loudspeaker.

A camera, set up perpendicular to the red convertible, to the actress's profile, shoots directly into the bank entrance in the background. In the doorway of the bank, two actors stand idly. They wear blue jeans and white cotton T-shirts and have nylon stockings pulled down to their brows. One of the young men has a blotch of red dye on his right knee to indicate that he's been shot. Evidence, Nolan supposes, of the love triangle Cosmo mentioned.

—Quiet on the set, the voice calls through the loudspeaker.

The actress tosses her cigarette and the two actors lower their nylon masks and walk inside the bank. In the commotion, Nolan notices Cosmo on the other side of the yellow cordon, wearing his press badge. Despite having been fired from the paper, he jots down notes and snaps photographs with the digital camera. No one seems to notice him or to care if they do.

—Marker.

Nolan hears a sharp smack of wood sticks, and then Maxine and the other young woman walk before the entrance to the bank as another extra, wearing overalls and a straw hat, tips his hat to them. A boy on a scooter swerves past.

A teenage girl standing beside Nolan raises her cell phone above the crowd of onlookers and pushes a button on the screen. Nolan hears the replicated sound of a camera shutter opening and closing to make the phone sound like an antique. The girl brings the phone down and looks at the image in the display screen. Then, she raises the phone again and again the shutter snaps.

Suddenly, the sound of a gunshot, muffled by the doors of the bank. A second later, the doors fling open and the man without the painted gunshot wound sprints to the convertible and dives in headfirst.

—Cut, the director yells.

Nolan watches Maxine and the other young woman laugh as they walk back to their original positions. He sees that

Cosmo is staring at Maxine and making no attempt to conceal his dejection. When she notices him, she looks away.

The actor who dove into the convertible pretends to struggle to get out of the vehicle, but he times his escape to coincide with Maxine walking by, arm in arm with the other woman. The man in the overalls and the boy on the scooter also return to their original positions. The actor says something to Maxine that makes her laugh; Nolan watches Cosmo watch this and seeing Cosmo witness Maxine flirting with the actor saddens him some. It also disappoints and angers him that his brother is this way. He doesn't approve of Cosmo being so public about his emotions. It's indecent and, ultimately, false. He's never been comfortable with his brother's need for attention. Even as children he thought that particular want unbecoming. It suggested a deeply layered miscalculation of how one ought to interact with the world. He took himself to the opposite extreme.

Nolan notices the shadow of his hat out before him.

But did you?

A light sprinkle of rain begins to fall. Nolan looks to the girl standing next to him, to the display on her phone. The picture is blurry because the sprinkles of rain magnify clusters of pixels into bright spindles of separate colors.

—Places, everyone, the voice says through the loudspeaker. We're losing daylight here.

Nolan watches them film the scene several times. Inside the bank, when the door swings open, he can see the actor who is pretending to be shot lying on the floor and reaching out to the convertible, to the female driver, perhaps, as the swinging doors slam shut on him.

—Quiet on the set.

Walking arm in arm with the other woman, Maxine smiles and laughs and flirts with the actor between takes. At one point, a woman scurries over to her and touches up her makeup. Someone from the crowd calls out to Maxine while this is happening, and she looks around the makeup artist and waves. Cosmo watches her throughout, adjusting his glasses now and then, his sense of rejection visible to all those around him, should they be looking.

The actors and extras are standing in position when the first crack of lightning strikes. Moments later, it begins to rain, lightly at first, and then a downpour.

A summer rain storm in northern California.

Members of the film crew hurry to cover the lights and camera. A man drives the convertible off the set. As the crowd disperses, Nolan watches dusty drops of water drip from the leaves of the trees around him. He can see Cosmo in the confusion, his glasses crooked. Maxine huddles under the awning of a storefront with the actor, the two of them laughing. Cosmo wipes rain from the pages of his notebook, pages where he's jotted down the thoughts in his head, the ink blurred by raindrops.

With his bandaged thumb, wet from the rain, pressed against his cheek, and his swollen black eye visible in his reflection in the phone-booth glass, Nolan waits through the rings, expecting to get Linda's answering machine. The streets are wet and black and glistening with colorful smears of reflected light. Cars pass, taking with them the light splash of tires on asphalt.

—Hi, you've reached Linda's answering machine. Please leave a message. Thank you.

Lightning flashes above Fumarole Peak to the north as

beads of rainwater run through the dust on the phone-booth glass. Nolan's jeans and shirt are soaking wet. He looks away from his eye in the reflection in the glass. He listens to the thunder roll.

Beep.

—Linda, it's Nolan.

He sighs, audibly.

—I can't come back down there. Not yet, but I will if that's where you're going to be, because I want to be with you. I want to talk with you. I like talking to you. I find it easy. And that's not often the case for me. I know you don't trust me, Linda, and I'm sorry I've given you reason not to. I'm sorry for leaving without saying why.

He sighs. The mountains to the north stand blue in the flashes of white light. The thunder gaining on the lightning cracks.

—I'd like to say you were the first I've done that to, but I'd be lying if I did, and you'd know it. I just want you to know you can trust me. Not right away. But I'll work for it. You'll see.

A truck drives past, similar in make and model to the one Guillermo and Manny drove, but a different color, its wipers swiping at the rain, its tires peeling water up from the road, shot with color from the signs and lights of the gas station and quick mart across the avenue.

—I can't get there anytime soon because my brother needs me. I swear that's not an excuse, Linda. I do. But I'd like to know if you'd see me again. I mean, I'm coming regardless, but I want to know if you'd see me for real, not just some late-night, now-and-then thing.

Lightning breaks over the edges of the town, illuminating the rooftops and power lines. Nolan sees light, cast off the wet road, shining along the undersides of the climbing irons set along either side of the knotted telephone pole. Then, thunder shakes the phone booth.

—I meant it when I asked you to come here. Everything I see makes me think of you. Of what I want to share with you. What I want to talk with you about. There's so much I need to talk to you about. I know I can get quiet, but I think you'd enjoy getting out up here and I'd enjoy being the one to show you around.

The connection clicks in his ear.

—Nolan, she says.

—Hey.

—Hey.

—How long have you been there?

—The entire time.

—Why didn't you pick up?

—I didn't think I should.

—Make me sweat some first.

—You deserve it.

—I do.

—Where are you?

—In a phone booth in front of this Chinese restaurant.

—It sounds like it's raining.

—It is.

He waits a second, then he says:

—What are you doing?

—I was reading.

—For school?

—No, I borrowed a novel from a friend.

—The guy you're seeing?

—No. A girlfriend.

Linda doesn't say more, so Nolan says:

—What's it about?

—San Francisco, actually.

—What's the story?

—This Chinese man during the Gold Rush brings his brother's remains to San Francisco so they can be shipped back home. But the sea captain throws the urn overboard once he sails through the Golden Gate. He throws a bunch of urns overboard.

—To lighten the ship's load, Nolan says.

—Pretty awful, right?

—That's what the book's about?

—So far.

A pause, then:

—Why are you reading that book?

—Like I said, I saw it at a friend's, and she said it was good.

—Maybe it's because it takes place in San Francisco. You were thinking about me.

She doesn't respond, but he can sense that she's smiling.

—I can't remember the last time I heard it rain, she says.

—Thunder and lightning, too.

—Hold the phone out so I can hear it.

—What?

—Hold the phone out. I want to hear the rain.

—OK.

Nolan opens the phone booth's accordion door and holds the receiver up to the sky and lightning cracks and rain falls down on the cold hard plastic. Rain falls on his sleeve and runs down his forearm.

—Could you hear it? he asks when he puts the phone back to the side of his head.

—It's beautiful.

—It smells good, too.

—I bet.

—You know what pennyroyal is?

—I do.

—There's some in a field near the booth. It smells like that.

—Nice.

He holds his free hand outside the booth and drops run cool along his bare arm. He can feel the rain fall on his cheeks.

—I miss you, Linda, he says.

—I miss you, too, she says.

12

Late morning of the next day Nolan wakes to the sound of an air tanker roaring over the rooftops of Valley Oaks, the plane's four 1,500-horsepower engines vibrating the glass of water on the garage floor beside his mattress.

When he steps into the hallway, he finds Cosmo's bedroom door open. The blinds in the room are drawn shut and the blankets are bundled at the foot of the bed in the same place Nolan saw them before he went to bed after midnight. Cosmo never came home, and the time on the alarm clock on the nightstand flashes, waiting to be reset.

While crossing the living room, the first thing Nolan notices through the sheer curtains of the picture window is a substantial column of smoke towering in the distance. He opens the front door and steps to the porch in his jeans and his bare feet and immediately he sees a neighbor standing in the street looking north, his hand pressed to his brow to shade his eyes. Nolan walks to the Valiant's oil spot in the concrete driveway.

—Wildfire, the man says to Nolan.

—Where?

—Fumarole Peak.

—Must've started with all the lightning.

—That's what they're saying on television.

—How many acres?

—Thousands so far.

—And it only started last night?

—That's what they're saying.

—What about containment?

—Not yet, the man says. This is going to be a big one.

Throughout the day, the column broadens and flattens with the shifting winds. It loses its definition as it spreads and shrouds the range of mountains. With time, smoke and ash descend upon Burnridge. The day's light takes on a sepia tone. Peach and orange hues. Autumn light. Beyond the shading leaves of Valley Oaks, the sun is a pale orb crossing the ash-white sky.

Nolan stays indoors reading and cleaning and waiting for Cosmo to return, while the acrid smell of wildfire smoke seeps through the spaces around the doors and windows and down the chimney flue. He dampens and rolls bath towels and arranges them along the bottoms of the doors leading outside to hold the world at bay, but the smell of the smoke finds its way into the house. He stands at the sliding glass door, watching flakes of ash fall on his tomato vines. He sees a neighbor on a rooftop wearing a full-face respirator and spraying the composite roofing with a garden hose, rivulets of water coursing through the fine ash toward the aluminum gutters.

At dusk, Nolan is sitting in the recliner with a handful of jumbled nails, arranging them one by one in his lap, trying to get them around the bandage on his thumb. The house phone rang earlier in the day and he heard their mother's voice on the answering machine in the kitchen and he listened to her say she'd heard about the fire on the news and that she hoped they were OK and if they needed a place to go to get away from the smoke for a few days that they were welcome to stay with her.

—I love you, boys, she said, with Nolan standing before the machine.

—I love you, too, Mom.

That night, just after dark, with smoke particles ferrying through the span of light cast by the front-porch lamp, a knock sounds at the door.

—I don't want to hear "I told you so," Joe says once Nolan's opened the door.

—All right.

—My wife's sister called. The cops have Mason on camera setting the bonfires down at Memorial Beach.

Nolan stiffens the muscles in his jaw and nods. Over Joe's shoulder, Nolan can see the Ram parked in the driveway. The engine is running, and heat, emanating from the grille, plays the smoke up in gentle gusts before the truck's headlights. The wipers swipe ash back and forth from the windshield.

—They don't know if he set them all, or if he's just a copycat, but they got him on camera.

—And no one knows where he's at now.

—No, Joe says, his arm free of the dishtowel sling. We're all out in this looking for him, and I figured you might have some ideas.

—I'll grab my boots.

They drive south along Burnridge Avenue, the town quiet and empty, layered with a fine dusting of ash. Tiny caps have formed on street-lamp globes and little ridges crown mailboxes.

—Sometimes I stop smelling it, Joe says, but I think that's just because I stop thinking about it.

—I know what you mean.

—My son almost puked; the smell is so strong out at our place.

—You have any masks?

—The hardware store was pretty well picked over by the time I got there.

—Dampen a handkerchief.

—That's what Maria did.

—Did it work?

—We should have done it earlier.

—You didn't know the wind would blow this way.

—No, but I just stood there, watching it come. I haven't been able to take my eyes off it.

—It's not something you see every day.

—No, it isn't.

—Yeah.

They pass a man walking hunched over while holding a washcloth to his face. He ventures from the sidewalk into the street, where some kids have heeled their names in the ash. Joe leans forward and looks up through the windshield.

—It's strange driving so slow through town, he says. Everything seems so different.

They come to a stop light at the car dealership. The insides of the cars are hollow with dark, and the decals on the windshields protrude slightly through the ash. On one windshield someone has written WATCH ME with their fingertip.

Nolan is thinking that the lack of ash in the lines of the letters means the words were written recently, when two shadowy figures, hunched close to the ground, skulk among the cars toward either end of an arch of balloons spanning a dozen automobiles.

—Nolan, Joe says calmly.

—I see them.

—What are they doing?

—I don't think they're trying to steal cars.

—Me neither.

The intersection light turns green, but Joe doesn't drive on until the figures have cut the arch free and the ends rise as the middle dips. The entire strand lifts through the smoke and slips into the gauzy dark like some giant, slow-moving bird.

—Man, Joe says, leaning over the steering wheel to see it better.

When Nolan looks back for the figures, they're gone. The signal light turns yellow, then red. Joe drives on.

Circling the plaza, they drive slowly past equipment left from where the bank robbery scene was filmed. Ash has settled in small drifts in front of blinking red signal lights, and lines the thresholds of the darkened plaza storefronts. It lingers on the painted lines of the road and dulls the reflector dots.

A station wagon, heavily laden with trunks and suitcases, drives toward the Ram with its windshield wipers flinging ash. Inside the car, a man and a woman with two children sitting between them on the bench seat. The children's eyes are wide open, the parents' eyes are tired and harried. Joe and Nolan raise their hands and the man and woman raise their hands back to them as the parties pass.

—You think they're coming down from it? Joe says.

—It sure looks that way. Nolan nods, his reflection in the side window lit by the clock on the truck's dash.

—I bet there's a hell of a view of this from the farmhouse, Joe says.

Nolan looks to Joe.

—Turn around, he says.

—Why?

—Because that's where he's at.

Driving up the gravel road to the farmhouse they can see patches of smoldering hot spots behind the fire line as it wends its way toward the crown of Fumarole Peak, the flames drawn along invisible contours like red and orange cursive on a black page.

—Wow, Joe says. Look at that.

Joe parks the truck before the trash heap and turns off the engine. Strips of metal and glass shine in the headlights like the eyes of critters staring back at them. A BMX bicycle leans against the oak where Nolan usually parks Cosmo's ex-wife's ten-speed.

When Joe notices Mason's bike, he reaches for the door handle and says:

—Son of a—

But Nolan places a hand on Joe's shoulder.

—Give me a minute first.

—He's dead.

—Just give me a minute with him first.

—Why? He's my nephew.

—Because the last thing he needs is someone yelling at him. He's got enough of that coming his way.

—What are you going to say to him?

—I don't know yet.

—Nolan—

—Joe, please. I called this. Please.

—All right. Joe nods.

The air in the house is thick with trapped smoke and ash. Without sheathing on the farmhouse roof, what light there is in the night seeps down the stairwell and makes the living room navigable. The floor was swept at the end of Friday's workday, and the materials they left behind are neatly arranged. The ladders, coated in a fine gray ash and chained to the exposed studs, lie on their sides next to one another. Cardboard boxes of nails pressed against one another in a corner, out of the way. A bucket of joist brackets. An empty trash can, lined with a fresh bag. The site is a tidy, organized space, fit for careful construction.

Nolan's only been to sleeping job sites a handful of times, and the stillness, where there's usually such commotion, pleases him, it speaks to his sense of order, as if the furnace of progress sometimes rests and cools before gathering its next heave.

At the top of the stairs, Nolan turns down the hallway toward the north-facing master bedroom. He makes his way carefully down the dark hallway, moving his hands at either side of him, from one stud to the next, all the old nails pulled from their faces, all the old wiring yanked from their sides. His fingertips find coarse holes where the insulated wires once ran, bearing electricity to wall switches that lit how many moments, in how many lives?

Nolan finds Mace in the master bedroom, sitting on an upturned five-gallon bucket staring at the wildfire, the darkened expanse of the valley floor spread out below. Nolan pauses at the door to gain his bearings, but then he walks forward to stand at the young man's side, at the side of a young self seriously contemplating its own existence in and absence from this world. A young self angry at the ways the world isn't because of the ways it never was.

Written across the face of Fumarole Peak, the lines of the fire mesmerize Nolan. He can see the heat shimmering. He can see the color consuming the black. He watches matter transform.

After a moment, Mace says:

—You ever seen anything like this?

—Once, a few years back, in New Mexico.

—I've never seen anything like it.

Mace raises a plastic bottle to his lower lip and spits tobacco juice into the mouth of the bottle.

—In school, I read that the natives used to burn out valleys so they would grow back stronger.

—I've heard that.

—I bet this knoll was something else then.

He shakes his head and spits into the bottle and then he just sits there, quietly staring ahead. Nolan leans against the window frame. He and Mason both have yet to take their eyes from the wildfire.

—What happened to your eye?

—I got in the middle of something.

—Looks like you got the worst of it.

—Tough to tell at this point.

—Why's that?

—Guy who hit me busted his wrist.

—Yeah, that's worse.

—But the guy he was aiming for could've used a good punch. A good punch might've served him better in the long run than not getting punched at all.

Mason spits.

—How'd you know where to find me?

—You light those fires in town?

The young man reaches up and scratches his cheek.

—Lightning did this, he points.

—I'm not asking you that.

Mason lowers his eyes to the floor. He nudges a stray nail on the floor with the toe of his boot. Without lifting his eyes, he says:

—Nobody got hurt.

—Not yet they didn't.

—Are you going to tell Joe?

—What, that I got suspicions?

—Yeah.

—I already did that.

—What'd he say?

—He didn't believe me.

—So why would he believe you now?

—He said they got you on camera.

Beyond the window, the blinking lights of a fire engine race across the valley, the lights skimming over the tops of the vineyard rows.

—You're making that up.

—I strike you as the type who'd make something like that up?

—To trick me, you might, yeah.

—I'm not the type to play tricks like that.

—How do I know that?

—Because I haven't shown you otherwise.

The lights on the engine run out over the vineyards but its siren is silent.

—There must've been more than one, Mason says.

—I don't know.

—I saw the one on the boat shack, but I went for it anyways.

The kid shakes his head as the truck disappears in the distance. Without lifting his eyes from the nail on the floor, Mason says:

—Do you think I'll go to jail?

—I can't say.

—What if I'm crazy?

—What do you mean?

—You know, plead insane.

—You're not insane.

Mason looks at Nolan, but Nolan continues to stare ahead.

—I only set the bonfires down at the river.

—It's not me you need to convince of that.

—They're not going to believe me, though.

—Probably not at first, no.

—You know why I did it?

—I do, Nolan nods.

—Why?

—Because you like how it feels. You like watching it happen. You like to see how others react to what you've made.

—Did you ever do it?

—No, but I know those feelings well.

A light, cool wind passes through the picture window. Mason looks up from the floor and out at the wildfire.

—Do you always wear that hat? he asks Nolan.

—I generally take it off before bed.

—No, I mean did you always wear it?

—No.

—Why'd you start?

—It keeps the sun out of my eyes.

—Lots of different hats to choose from. Why that one?

—Because I like how it makes me look.

—But you weren't always this way, were you?

—No.

—You think you always will be?

—No.

—I was never with that girl, Mason says then. The one I told you about. I lied about that. I was trying to impress you.

Nolan sets a hand on the kid's shoulder.

—Joe's waiting on us.

13

After leaving the farmhouse, Joe and Nolan drive Mason to the Burnridge police station to meet his mother and the lawyer she called. With word out that the police have a suspect in the arsons, news crews have posted up outside the station. With all the smoke from the fire, they sit in their vehicles wearing masks. Pulling up to the station, Nolan notices the vans. He sees one man in a mask sleeping against the driver's-side window of the van he's in.

—Vultures, Joe says.

—Drive around back, Nolan says to Joe.

Nolan gets out and slips past the sleeping news people and into the reception area. A cameraman sleeps in a chair in the waiting area, his camera at his feet, the lens a glossy, charcoal-colored eye, drowsing. Nolan walks quietly up to the bullet-proof partition and the night dispatch gets up from her desk and walks over and presses a button on the microphone on her side and says loudly:

—Yes?

Speaking softly so as not to wake the sleeping cameraman, Nolan says:

—The boy you all are looking for is around back.

—Who?

—The boy—

—Speak up, please.

The reporter stirs. Nolan looks in the woman's eyes.

—Are you all right? she asks him. Is this an emergency?

Nolan leans forward to speak into the microphone on his side of the partition.

—I'm trying to do this without creating a scene, he says.

—Do what?

—Help.

With Mason in custody, Joe drives Nolan home. He stops in front of Cosmo's driveway, behind the Valiant, and puts the Ram in park.

—I figure we should wait a day or so before starting back up, Joe says.

—Yeah, all right.

Music, playing outside, thumps faintly over the diesel engine. As Nolan reaches for the door handle, Joe says:

—I'm sorry I didn't hear what you said the other day.

—I should have been more clear in what I was saying.

—You didn't know enough to accuse him of it?

—No.

—Well, thanks for at least trying.

—You would have done the same.

—No, I probably would have accused the little shit without any evidence.

Nolan opens the truck door and immediately the loud and discordant music sounds from the house down the way. The front door to the house is open and ash somersaults through the porch light and settles over the concrete porch and the lawn.

—Sounds like a rager, Joe says.

—Sounds like it, Nolan responds, still looking at the illuminated doorway and knowing somehow that Cosmo is associated with it standing open like that, with the bright light shining within.

Joe extends his hand.

—Thanks, Nolan.

They shake.

—No worries.

—No worries? Joe smiles.

—It's all good.

—I'll see you later.

—Bye now.

—Adios.

After watching Joe's taillights disappear, Nolan turns to Cosmo's house, where the Valiant is parked in the driveway at an angle, the tires cranked hard to the side. Ash has lightly filled the track marks, the steps heading into the house, and those coming back out and going down the street toward the open door.

Nolan walks inside Cosmo's house and when he opens the door to the garage, he finds the cardboard boxes un-stacked and kitchen utensils, pots and pans, oven mitts, placemats, and chopping blocks strewn about the room. In the middle of all this, Nolan notices the fireproof box is open on the love seat and the .38 and the six cartridges are gone.

As he sprints down the street, his footsteps land occasionally in ones made earlier by Cosmo, and each footfall stomps ash into air thick with smoke. Nolan slows as he approaches the front porch. Music blasts through the bright doorway. Peering around the door jamb, he sees a middle-aged woman slumped over a dining-room table, her head resting on her arms. She sits beneath a brass chandelier outfitted with light bulbs made to resemble candles. A mess of beer bottles and wine glasses and shot glasses surrounds her. A cookie sheet of seasoned potato strips sits at the center of the table, a smeared dollop of ketchup pushed toward the corner of the sheet. Nolan sees the woman's shoulders rise and fall with each breath she takes. He crosses the threshold.

The sound is tremendous about him as he steps from the tiled foyer to the living room. A swath of beige carpet, heavily stained by foot traffic, leads toward a staircase, where a pair of sneakers lie upended at the bottom of the staircase. Clothes are strewn over the floor, over the back of the couch where Cosmo sits, his feet propped on a coffee table littered with alcohol bottles and cigarette butts, pizza crusts and deep-fried jalapeño poppers.

Cosmo has the gun in one hand and a beer in the other and he is aiming the gun at the sliding glass door across the room and talking to himself. The patio is dark beyond the glass, and the door vividly reflects the room's interior, with Cosmo at its center. When Cosmo sees Nolan slip into the reflection in the sliding glass door, he smiles and raises the beer bottle and yells:

—If you can't beat them, join them.

Nolan steps over to the jumbo entertainment console and turns down the volume on the receiver until the house is completely quiet.

—You missed a good one, Cosmo says loudly, his hearing having not adjusted yet to the quiet. Kids these days, he says, they do it right. They go for broke.

Nolan steps forward and extends his hand to his brother.

—Give me back my gun, Cosmo.

—No, I'm good. I don't want to leave yet.

Nolan stands before his brother, his hand extended and open.

—Anyone see you with that?

—No, I took it out after they left for more tequila.

—You need to meet me halfway on this one, Cosmo.

—I'm fine, dude. Grab a beer from the fridge. Everyone's coming back. I'll put it away before they get here.

Nolan looks Cosmo in the eye until Cosmo looks down and away.

—That doesn't belong to you, Cosmo.

—I was looking for a spatula. I was going to throw pancakes over the fence at them, like discs.

—What did you plan on doing with it?

Cosmo rolls the .38 from side to side using his wrist, his hand beneath and then on top of it. With his eyes on the handgun, he says, meekly:

—I don't know.

—Give it back, Cosmo. Dad gave me that.

—You ever wonder why he gave you a gun and me a lighter?

—I don't know why.

Cosmo lifts his eyes to Nolan's.

—He told me once the lighter saved his life. Did you know that?

—No.

—Of course.

Nolan watches his brother's brow unfurrow as his tired, sad eyes return to the gun.

—You weren't there when he got talkative at the end.

Nolan curls and uncurls his fingers.

—Give it here, Cos.

—He was in a foxhole. At night. He said he and the guy he was with hadn't been "in country" for more than a week. Apparently, he lit a cigarette with this very lighter, and then passed it over to the guy, still lit, and a sniper blew the guy's brains out. Dad said he spent the entire night in the foxhole with some dead guy's brains all over the place.

—I didn't know that.

—He said he never told anyone what happened, he was so ashamed.

Nolan slides his teeth over each other, back and forth, lightly, his hand still extended, but lowered some.

—I remember, Cosmo says, when I was a kid, how the two of you would stay up late watching westerns. I could hear the gunshots from down the hall and I would get so mad because I couldn't concentrate on my reading.

—You could've watched with us.

—Really? Could I? Thanks.

Cosmo closes his eyes and shakes his head.

—What if I didn't want to? What if I wanted to read in peace and quiet? What if I wanted all of us to sit around and read?

—You were always different than the rest of us. Better, even.

—Boy genius, Cosmo scoffs. I think he thought I was gay.

—What?

—Because I would rather read than watch westerns with you guys.

—That's all in your head, Cosmo.

Cosmo looks down at the gun.

—They traveled all that way just to die.

—Who did?

—The Russians.

Quietly, Cosmo adds:

—At the end, I thought he might get better.

—I'm sorry I wasn't there.

—You should have been. Cosmo nods, more with his shoulders than his chin.

—I know. I was wrong not to.

Cosmo rubs the handle of the .38 with his thumb and the snub-nosed barrel droops toward the carpet.

—When I got home tonight, I thought you'd left. I thought you'd left, too.

—I'm not going anywhere.

—She said I'm obsessed.

—Who did?

—Dawn. She said I was obsessed with everything but her. That's why she left me.

Cosmo looks up at Nolan and his eyes are red-rimmed and puffy. Scared.

—I think I'm going crazy, Nolan.

—You're not crazy. You're a mess, but you're not crazy.

—You think? He smiles.

—I know.

—I'm sorry that guy hit you, Cosmo says.

—I know you are.

—I mean, I'm not sorry I didn't get punched, but I'm sorry you did.

Nolan smiles a crooked smile and shakes his head.

—Give me my gun back, smartass.

Cosmo looks Nolan in the eye and he hands him the gun. Nolan tucks the snub-nosed revolver in the waistband of his blue jeans at the small of his back and then he extends his hand once again.

—All right, Cosmo says, taking his brother's hand. But not too fast, or I'll be sick.

Nolan helps Cosmo from the couch, helps steady his brother where he stands.

—I did shots with the mom, Cosmo says as they cross the foyer. Apparently, she parties with the kids to keep an eye on them.

Nolan closes the front door behind them, and Valley Oaks is as quiet as he has ever heard it. They walk side by side up the middle of the street. Nolan has his hands in his pockets and Cosmo scratches at his head. Nolan can see his footprints in the ash from when Joe dropped him off. He can see his footprints from when he ran down the street. He can see the parallels of Joe's tires running down the street, in and out of the street lamps, in and out of pools of light filled with swirling flakes, in and out of lines and decisions and actions and indecisions and memories and remnants of memories yet.

On the walkway leading to Cosmo's front porch, Cosmo says:

—It's time to burn this place to the ground. Collect the insurance money before the bank forecloses on us.

—How much do you need?

—More than I have.

—Yeah, well, I might be able to help out with that some.

—Your insurance check came through.

—Yes, it did.

—I know. I saw the envelope in the mail.

—Then why ask?

—I wasn't asking. It was a simple declarative sentence.

Two weeks later, alone on the job site, Nolan crawls beneath the farmhouse, holding the droplight out before him. Several days earlier Joe noticed a creak in the kitchen subfloor, and so now Nolan is carrying the worm-drive saw, his tape, square, hammer, and a handful of nails out to reinforce the subfloor with blocking.

The light and the tools make the crawling difficult. Nolan has to keep below the new plumbing and electrical work while navigating his way around a recently installed network of insulated heating and cooling ducts. Every now and then he has to stop to gently yank the droplight's cord free of brittle snags in the concrete footings, and the action sends odd and jarring shadows through the stubborn dark.

When he gets to the area beneath the kitchen, he rolls over on his back and sinks a sixteen in a joist two bays over from where he needs to install the blocks. He hangs the light from the nail and by it he takes his measurements. He measures twice and he cuts once. Then, he wedges the cut blocks in by hand and taps them in place with his hammer and nails them fast. He reaches up and tests them by hand. Solid pieces of clear fir held tight up against the plywood subfloor between beautiful, old, true-dimension redwood joists.

Finished with the task, Nolan rests for a moment, letting his eyes wander over everything they did that summer: the new green board posts, the stem wall, the seismic sheer paneling, the galvanized brackets bolted down tight. Much of it his and Manny's work. The low men.

The wildfire burned for five days straight, the wind blowing ash and smoke over the town on some days, and from it on others. On one of those days, a house fire started downtown. The arsonist's remains were found inside, lying on the floor on the way toward a bicycle, outfitted with panniers, that was parked on the back porch. In the panniers, glass jars of gasoline.

The remains were never identified. A nameless man consumed by his methods, his reasons never to be known.

Reaching for the droplight, Nolan notices a signature, written in pencil, on the flat side of a new fir joist:

Guillermo Del Caminoreal

The quiet carpenter who signs his work where few, if anyone, will notice.

When he meets Linda at the Sonoma County Airport, the last traces of his black eye are faint, but still there, waiting for her approval.

—Nice, she says, reaching up to touch it, but stopping short. You want to tell me about it now or keep it in your arsenal until I'm furious with you and ready to leave?

—What makes you so sure I'm going to make you furious?

—You're right. I won't let that happen again.

Nolan looks down and away from her eyes but he takes her hands in his own.

—I'm sorry, Linda. I'm glad you're here and I'm sorry.

—You're lucky I'm here. You know that, right?

He looks back into her eyes.

—I do.

—Don't fuck it up.

He pulls her close and they hug and he holds her for some time, smelling her and remembering how she feels in his arms. When they separate, Nolan grabs the handle to her suitcase and they walk across the nearly empty parking lot toward Cosmo's Valiant.

—Where's your truck? she asks.

—Part of the same story.

On the way to the ocean, they drive the Valiant through canted bars of hazy light that penetrate the cool dark of a densely wooded stretch of back road. Linda sits with her hand resting between them on the bench seat, a hand he wants to hold but he's nervous in a way he hasn't been since he was a teenager, so he doesn't.

When they near the ocean, she rolls down the window all the way and leans her head out into the rushing wind and turns her face up at the sky.

Don't fuck it up. He smiles to himself.

They emerge from the redwood forest into old cattle land, a jumble of old sea floor uplifted by subduction and terraced by hooves. Dotted with serpentine outcrops. Flaxen-colored hillsides folding over one another on their way down to the blue of the Pacific Ocean. Nolan turns on to the coastal highway, and drives south along the edge of the continent. Before long he pulls the Valiant into an asphalt turnout overlooking the ocean and parks at the head of a footpath that leads down to a sandy beach. A flock of seagulls weaves tight weaves overhead in one giant, revolving mass.

—Maybe we should sit here a minute. Linda smiles.

—I hear you.

The vast expanse of the Pacific lies before them, and rack upon rack of cresting waves crash on the sandy beach and spread out over the wet sand. Linda leans forward and looks across Nolan.

—What are you looking at? he asks.

—How far is the Golden Gate from here?

—I don't know, about an hour or so. Why, you want to go?

—Not yet. I was just thinking about those urns.

She sits back and looks west.

—It was a good idea to come out here, she says.

—Yeah.

—"Yeah." She shakes her head, smiling.

A string of automobile traffic passes the turnout. Nolan and Linda sit comfortably with the wind rushing around the Valiant while gull shadows cross dark troughs of the waves, cross the coruscating spindrift. Linda scoots across the bench seat and Nolan raises his arm and settles it around her shoulder as she rests against him, placing her hand on his thigh. After a moment, she looks at him and smiles, and then she looks out over the ocean through the Valiant's dusty windshield.

—I can't wait to kiss you again, he says.

Without looking toward him, she says:

—So don't.